There was a knock at the door and Mary opened it, supposing, of course, that it was the bell-boy with a pitcher of ice-water, for which she had just rung.

"Ah, here you are at last, my pretty Mary!" It was the voice of her pursuer that menaced her, with all the stored-up wrath of his long-baffled search.

For an instant it seemed to Mary that she was going to faint, and in one swift flash of thought she saw herself being overpowered and carried away into hiding before Tryon, her friend and protector, could return . . .

Grace
LIVINGSTON HILL

AMERICA'S BEST-LOVED STORYTELLER

THE
MYSTERY
OF MARY

LIVING BOOKS®
Tyndale House Publishers, Inc.
Wheaton, Illinois

This Tyndale House book
by Grace Livingston Hill
contains the complete text
of the original hardcover edition.
NOT ONE WORD
HAS BEEN OMITTED.

Living Books is a registered trademark of Tyndale House
Publishers, Inc.

Library of Congress Catalog Card Number 89-50880
ISBN 0-8423-4632-5

Printed in the United States of America

00 99 98 97 96 95
 9   8   7   6

HE paused on the platform and glanced at his watch. The train on which he had just arrived was late. It hurried away from the station, and was swallowed up in the blackness of the tunnel, as if it knew its own shortcomings and wished to make up for them.

It was five minutes of six, and as the young man looked back at the long flight of steps that led to the bridge across the tracks, a delicate pencilling of electric light flashed into outline against the city's deepening dusk, emphasizing the lateness of the hour. He had a dinner engagement at seven, and it was yet some distance to his home, where a rapid toilet must be made if he were to arrive on time.

The stairway was long, and there were many people thronging it. A shorter cut led down along the tracks under the bridge, and up the grassy embankment. It would bring him a whole block nearer home, and a line of cabs was standing over at the corner just above the bridge. It was against the rules to walk beside the tracks—there was a large sign to that effect in front of him—but it would save five minutes. He scanned the platform hastily to see if any officials were in sight, then bolted down the darkening tracks.

Under the centre of the bridge a slight noise behind him, as of soft, hurrying footsteps, caught his attention, and a woman's voice broke upon his startled senses.

"Please don't stop nor look around," it said, and the owner caught up with him now in the shadow. "But will you kindly let me walk beside you for a moment, till you can show me how to get out of this dreadful place? I am very much frightened, and I'm afraid I shall be followed. Will you tell where I can go to hide?"

After an instant's astonished pause, he obeyed her and kept on, making room for her to walk beside him, while he took the place next to the tracks. He was aware, too, of the low rumble of a train, coming from the mouth of the tunnel.

His companion had gasped for breath, but began again in a tone of apology:

"I saw you were a gentleman, and I didn't know what to do. I thought you would help me to get somewhere quickly."

Just then the fiery eye of the oncoming train burst from the tunnel ahead. Instinctively, the young man caught his companion's arm and drew her forward to the embankment beyond the bridge, holding her, startled and trembling, as the screaming train tore past them.

The pent black smoke from the tunnel rolled in a thick cloud about them, stifling them. The girl, dazed with the roar and blinded by the smoke, could only cling to her protector. For an instant they felt as if they were about to be drawn into the awful power of the rushing monster. Then it had passed, and a roar of silence followed, as if they were suddenly plunged into a vacuum. Gradually the noises of the world began again: the rumble of a trolley-car on the bridge; the "honk-honk" of an automobile; the cry of a newsboy. Slowly their breath and their senses came back.

The man's first thought was to get out of the cut before another train should come. He grasped his companion's arm and started up the steep embankment, realizing as he did so that the wrist he held was slender, and that the sleeve which covered it was of the finest cloth.

They struggled up, scarcely pausing for breath. The steps at the side of the bridge, made for the convenience of railroad hands, were out of the question, for they were at a dizzy height, and hung unevenly over the yawning pit where trains shot constantly back and forth.

As they emerged from the dark, the man saw that his companion was a young and beautiful woman, and that she wore a light cloth gown, with neither hat nor gloves.

At the top of the embankment they paused, and the girl, with her hand at her throat, looked backward with a shudder. She seemed like a young bird that could scarcely tell which way to fly.

Without an instant's hesitation, the young man raised his hand and hailed a four-wheeler across the street.

"Come this way, quick!" he urged, helping her in. He gave the driver his home address and stepped in after her. Then, turning, he faced his companion, and was suddenly keenly aware of the strange situation in which he had placed himself.

"Can you tell me what is the matter," he asked, "and where you would like to go?"

The girl had scarcely recovered breath from the long climb and the fright, and she answered him in broken phrases.

"No, I cannot tell you what is the matter,"—she paused and looked at him, with a sudden comprehension of what he might be thinking about her—"but—there is nothing—that is—I have done nothing wrong——" She paused again and looked up with eyes whose clear depths, he felt, could hide no guile.

"Of course," he murmured with decision, and then wondered why he felt so sure about it.

"Thank you," she said. Then, with frightened perplexity: "I don't know where to go. I never was in this city before. If you will kindly tell me how to get somewhere— I suppose to a railroad station—and yet—no, I have no money—and"—then with a sudden little movement of dismay—"and I have no hat! Oh!"

The young man felt a strong desire to shield this girl so unexpectedly thrown on his mercy. Yet vague fears hovered about the margin of his judgment. Perhaps she was a thief or an adventuress. It might be that he ought to let her get out of the odd situation she appeared to be in, as best she might. Yet even as the thought flashed through his mind he seemed to hear an echo of her words, "I saw you were a gentleman," and he felt incapable of betraying her trust in him.

The girl was speaking again: "But I must not trouble you any more. You have been very kind to get me out of that dreadful place. If you will just stop the carriage and let me out, I am sure I can take care of myself."

"I could not think of letting you get out here alone. If you are in danger, I will help you." The warmth of his own words startled him. He knew he ought to be more cautious with a stranger, but impetuously he threw caution to the winds. "If you would just tell me a little bit about it, so that I should know what I ought to do for you——"

"Oh, I must not tell you! I couldn't!" said the girl, her hand fluttering up to her heart, as if to hold its wild beating from stifling her. "I am sorry to have involved you for a moment in this. Please let me out here. I am not frightened, now that I got away from that terrible tunnel. I was afraid I might have to go in there alone, for I didn't see any way to get up the bank, and I couldn't go back."

"I am glad I happened to be there," breathed the young man fervently. "It would have been dangerous for you to enter that tunnel. It runs an entire block. You would probably have been killed."

The girl shut her eyes and pressed her fingers to them. In the light of the street lamps, he saw that she was very white, and also that there were jewels flashing from the rings on her fingers. It was apparent that she was a lady of wealth and refinement. What could have brought her to this pass?

The carriage came to a sudden stop, and, looking out, he saw they had reached his home. A new alarm seized him as the girl moved as if to get out. His dignified mother and his fastidious sister were probably not in, but if by any chance they should not have left the house, what would they think if they saw a strange, hatless young woman descend from the carriage with him? Moreover, what would the butler think?

"Excuse me," he said, "but, really, there are reasons why I shouldn't like you to get out of the carriage just here. Suppose you sit still until I come out. I have a dinner engagement and must make a few changes in my dress, but it will take me only a few minutes. You are in no danger, and I will take you to some place of safety. I will try to think what to do while I am gone. On no account get out of the carriage. It would make the driver suspicious, you know. If you are really followed, he will let no one disturb you in the carriage, of course. Don't distress yourself. I'll hurry. Can you give me the address of any friend to whom I might 'phone or telegraph?"

She shook her head and there was a glitter of tears in her eyes as she replied:

"No, I know of no one in the city who could help me."

"I will help you, then," he said with sudden resolve, and in a tone that would be a comfort to any woman in distress.

His tone and the look of respectful kindliness he gave her kept the girl in the carriage until his return, although in her fear and sudden distrust of all the world, she thought more than once of attempting to slip away. Yet without money, and in a costume which could but lay her open to suspicion, what was she to do? Where was she to go?

As the young man let himself into his home with his latch-key, he heard the butler's well trained voice answering the telephone.

"Yes, ma'am; this is Mrs. Dunham's residence. . . . No, ma'am, she is not at home. . . . No, ma'am, Miss Dunham is out also. . . . Mr. Dunham? Just wait a moment, please. I think Mr. Dunham has just come in. Who shall I say wishes to speak to him? . . . Mrs. Parker Bowman? . . . Yes, ma'am; just wait a minute, please. I'll call Mr. Dunham."

The young man frowned. Another interruption! And Mrs. Bowman! It was at her house that he was to dine. What could the woman want? Surely it was not so late that she was looking him up. But perhaps something had happened, and she was calling off her dinner. What luck if she was! Then he would be free to attend the problem of the young woman whom fate, or Providence, had suddenly thrust upon his care.

He took the receiver, resolved to get out of going to the dinner if it were possible.

"Good evening, Mrs. Bowman."

"Oh, is that you, Mr. Dunham? How relieved I am! I am in a bit of difficulty about my dinner, and called up to see if your sister couldn't help me out. Miss Mayo has failed me. Her sister has had an accident, and she cannot leave her. She has just 'phoned me, and I don't know what to do. Isn't Cornelia at home? Couldn't you persuade her to come and help me out? She would have been invited in Miss Mayo's place if she had not told me that she expected to go to Boston this week. But she changed her plans, didn't she? Isn't she where you could reach her by 'phone and beg her to come and help me out? You see, it's a very particular dinner, and I've made all my arrangements."

"Well, now, that's too bad, Mrs. Bowman," began the young man, thinking he saw a way out of both their difficulties. "I'm sorry Cornelia isn't here. I'm sure she would do anything in her power to help you. But she and mother were to dine in Chestnut Hill to-night, and they must have left the house half an hour ago. I'm afraid she's out of the question. Suppose you leave me out? You won't have any trouble then except to take two plates off the table"—he laughed pleasantly—"and you would have even couples. You see," he hastened to add, as he heard Mrs. Parker Bowman's preliminary dissent—"you see, Mrs. Bowman, I'm in somewhat of a predicament myself. My train was late, and as I left the station I happened to meet a young woman—a—a friend." (He reflected rapidly on the old proverb, "A friend in need is a friend indeed." In that sense she was a friend.) "She is temporarily separated from her friends, and is a stranger in the city. In fact, I'm the only acquaintance or friend she has, and I feel rather under obligation to see her to her hotel and look up trains for her. She leaves the city to-night."

"Now, look here, Tryon Dunham, you're not going to leave me in the lurch for any young woman. I don't care how old an acquaintance she is! You simply bring her along. She'll make up my number and relieve me wonderfully. No, don't you say a word. Just tell her that she needn't stand on ceremony. Your mother and I are too old friends for that. Any friend of yours is a friend of mine, and my house is open to her. She won't mind. These girls who have travelled a great deal learn to step over the little formalities of calls and introductions. Tell her I'll call on her afterwards, if she'll only remain in town long enough, or I'll come and take dinner with her when I happen to be in her city. I suppose she's just returned from abroad—they all have—or else she's just going—and if she hasn't learned to accept things as she finds them, she probably will soon. Tell her what a plight I'm in, and that it will be a real blessing to me if she'll come. Besides—I didn't mean to tell you—I meant it for a surprise, but I may as well tell you now—Judge Blackwell is to be here, with his wife, and I especially want you to meet him. I've been trying to get you two together for a long time."

"Ah!" breathed the young man, with interest. "Judge Blackwell! I have wanted to meet him."

"Well, he has heard about you, too, and I think he wants to meet you. Did you know he was thinking of taking a partner into his office? He has always refused—but that's another story, and I haven't time to talk. You ought to be on your way here now. Tell your friend I will bless her forever for helping me out, and I won't take no for an answer. You said she'd just returned from abroad, didn't you? Of course she's musical. You must make her give us some music. She will, won't she? I was depending on Miss Mayo for that this evening."

"Well, you might be able to persuade her," murmured the distracted young man at the 'phone, as he struggled with one hand to untie his necktie and unfasten his collar, and mentally calculated how long it would take him to get into his dress suit.

"Yes, of course. You'd better not speak of it—it might make her decline. And don't let her stop to make any changes in her dress. Everybody will understand when I tell them she's just arrived—didn't you say?—from the other side, and we caught her on the wing. There's some one coming now. Do, for pity's sake, hurry, Tryon, for my cook is terribly cross when I hold up a dinner too long.

Good-by. Oh, by the way, what did you say was her name?"

"Oh-ah!" He had almost succeeded in releasing his collar, and was about to hang up the receiver, when this new difficulty confronted him.

"Oh, yes, of course; her name—I had almost forgotten," he went on wildly, to make time, and searched about in his mind for a name—any name—that might help him. The telephone book lay open at the r's. He pounced upon it and took the first name his eye caught.

"Yes—why—Remington, Miss Remington."

"Remington!" came in a delighted scream over the phone. "Not Carolyn Remington? That would be too good luck!"

"No," he murmured distractedly; "no, not Carolyn. Why, I—ah—I think—Mary—Mary Remington."

"Oh, I'm afraid I haven't met her, but never mind. Do hurry up, Tryon. It is five minutes of seven. Where did you say she lives?" But the receiver was hung up with a click, and the young man tore up the steps to his room three at a bound. Dunham's mind was by no means at rest. He felt that he had done a tremendously daring thing, though, when he came to think of it, he had not suggested it himself; and he did not quite see how he could get out of it, either, for how was he to have time to help the girl if he did not take her with him?

Various plans floated through his head. He might bring her into the house, and make some sort of an explanation to the servants, but what would the explanation be? He could not tell them the truth about her, and how would he explain the matter to his mother and sister? For they might return before he did, and would be sure to ask innumerable questions.

And the girl—would she go with him? If not, what should he do with her? And about her dress? Was it such as his "friend" could wear to one of Mrs. Parker Bowman's exclusive dinners? To his memory, it seemed quiet and refined. Perhaps that was all that was required for a woman who was travelling. There it was again! But he had not said she was travelling, nor that she had just returned from abroad, nor that she was a musician. How could he answer such questions about an utter stranger, and yet how could he not answer them, under the circumstances?

And she wore no hat, nor cloak. That would be a strange way to arrive at a dinner. How could she accept? He was settling his coat into place when a queer little bulge attracted his attention to an inside pocket. Impatiently he pulled out a pair of long white gloves. They were his sister's, and he now remembered she had given them to him to carry the night before, on the way home from a reception, she having removed them because it was raining. He looked at them with a sudden inspiration. Of course! Why had he not thought of that? He hurried into his sister's room to make a selection of a few necessities for the emergency—only to have his assurance desert him at the very threshold. The room was immaculate, with no feminine finery lying about. Cornelia Dunham's maid was well trained. The only article that seemed out of place was a hand-box on a chair near the door. It bore the name of a fashionable milliner, and across the lid was pencilled in Cornelia's large, angular hand, "To be returned to Madame Dollard's." He caught up the box and strode over to the closet. There was no time to lose, and this box doubtless contained a hat of some kind. If it was to be returned, Cornelia would think it had been called for, and no further inquiry would be made about the matter. He could call at Madame's and settle the bill without his sister's knowledge.

He poked back into the closet and discovered several wraps and evening cloaks of more or less elaborate style, but the thought came to him that perhaps one of these would be recognized as Cornelia's. He closed the door hurriedly and went down to a large closet under the stairs, from which he presently emerged with his mother's new black rain-coat. He patted his coat-pocket to be sure he had the gloves, seized his hat, and hurried back to the carriage, the hat-box in one hand and his mother's rain-coat dragging behind him. His only anxiety was to get out before the butler saw him.

As he closed the door, there flashed over him the sudden possibility that the girl had gone. Well, perhaps that would be the best thing that could happen and would save him a lot of trouble; yet to his amazement he found that the thought filled him with a sense of disappointment. He did not want her to be gone. He peered anxiously into the carriage, and was relieved to find her still there, huddled into the shadow, her eyes looking large and frightened. She was seized with a fit of trembling, and it required all her strength to keep him from noticing it. She was half afraid of the man, now that she had waited for him. Perhaps he was not a gentleman, after all.

2

"I am afraid I have been a long time," he said apologetically, as he closed the door of the carriage, after giving Mrs. Parker Bowman's address to the driver. In the uncertain light of the distant arc-lamp, the girl looked small and appealing. He felt a strong desire to lift her burdens and carry them on his own broad shoulders.

"I've brought some things that I thought might help," he said. "Would you like to put on this coat? It may not be just what you would have selected, but it was the best I could find that would not be recognized. The air is growing chilly."

He shook out the coat and threw it around her.

"Oh, thank you," she murmured gratefully, slipping her arms into the sleeves.

"And this box has some kind of a hat, I hope," he went on. "I ought to have looked, but there really wasn't time." He unknotted the strings and produced a large picture hat with long black plumes. He was relieved to find it black. While he untied the strings, there had been a growing uneasiness lest the hat be one of those wild, queer combinations of colors that Cornelia frequently purchased and called "artistic."

The girl received the hat with a grateful relief that was entirely satisfactory to the young man.

"And now," said he, as he pulled out the gloves and laid them gravely in her lap, "we're invited out to dinner."

"Invited out to dinner!" gasped the girl.

"Yes. It's rather a providential thing to have happened, I think. The telephone was ringing as I opened the door, and Mrs. Parker Bowman, to whose house I was invited, was asking for my sister to fill the place of an absent guest. My sister is away, and I tried to beg off. I told her I had accidentally met I hope you will pardon me—I called you a friend."

"Oh!" she said. "That was kind of you."

"I said you were a stranger in town, and as I was your only acquaintance, I felt that I should show you the courtesy of taking you to a hotel, and assisting to get you off on the night train; and I asked her to excuse me, as that would give her an even number. But it seems she had invited some one especially to meet me, and was greatly distressed not to have her full quota of guests, so she sent you a most cordial invitation to come to her at once, promising to take dinner with you some time if you would help her out now. Somehow, she gathered from my talk that you were travelling, had just returned from abroad, and were temporarily separated from your friends. She is also sure that you are musical, and means to ask you to help her out in that way this evening. I told her I was not sure whether you could be persuaded or not, and she mercifully refrained from asking whether you sang or played. I tell you all this so that you will be prepared for anything. Of course I didn't tell her all these things. I merely kept still when she inferred them. Your name, by the way, is Miss Remington—Mary Remington. She was greatly elated for a moment when she thought you might be Carolyn

Remington—whoever she may be. I suppose she will speak of it. The name was the first one that my eye lit upon in the telephone-book. If you object to bearing it for the evening, it is easy to see how a name could be misunderstood over the 'phone. But perhaps you would better give me a few pointers, for I've never tried acting a part, and can't be sure how well I shall do it."

The girl had been silent from astonishment while the man talked.

"But I cannot possibly go there to dinner," she gasped, her hand going to her throat again, as if to pluck away the delicate lace about it and give more room for breathing. "I must get away somewhere at once. I cannot trouble you in this way. I have already imposed upon your kindness. With this hat and coat and gloves, I shall be able to manage quite well, and I thank you so much! I will return them to you as soon as possible."

The cab began to go slowly, and Tryon Dunham noticed that another carriage, just ahead of theirs, was stopping before Mrs. Bowman's house. There was no time for halting decision.

"My friend," he said earnestly, "I cannot leave you alone, and I do not see a better way than for you to go in here with me for a little while, till I am free to go with you. No one can follow you here, or suspect that you had gone out to dinner at a stranger's house. Believe me, it is the very safest thing you could do. This is the house. Will you go in with me? If not, I must tell the driver to take us somewhere else."

"But what will she think of me," she said in trepidation, "and how can I do such a thing as to steal into a woman's house to a dinner in this way! Besides, I am not dressed for a formal occasion."

The carriage had stopped before the door now, and the driver was getting down from his seat.

"Indeed, she will think nothing about it," Dunham

assured her, "except to be glad that she has the right number of guests. Her dinners are delightful affairs usually, and you have nothing to do but talk about impersonal matters for a little while and be entertaining. She was most insistent that you take no thought about the matter of dress. She said it would be perfectly understood that you were travelling, and that the invitation was unexpected. You can say that your trunk has not come, or has gone on ahead. Will you come?"

Then the driver opened the carriage door.

In an instant the girl assumed the self-contained manner she had worn when she had first spoken to him. She stepped quietly from the carriage, and only answered in a low voice, "I suppose I'd better, if you wish it."

Dunham paused for a moment to give the driver a direction about carrying the great pasteboard box to his club. This idea had come as a sudden inspiration. He had not thought of the necessity of getting rid of that box before.

"If it becomes necessary, where shall I say you are going this evening?" he asked in a low tone, as they turned to go up the steps. She summoned a faint, flickering smile.

"When people have been travelling abroad and are stopping over in this city, they often go on to Washington, do they not?" she asked half shyly.

He smiled in response, and noted with pleasure that the black hat was intensely becoming. She was not ill-dressed for the part she had to play, for the black silk raincoat gave the touch of the traveller to her costume.

The door swung open before they could say another word, and the young man remembered that he must introduce his new friend. As there was no further opportunity to ask her about her name, he must trust to luck.

The girl obeyed the motion of the servant and slipped up to the dressing-room as if she were a frequent guest in the house, but it was in some trepidation that Tryon Dunham removed his overcoat and arranged his necktie. He had caught a passing glimpse of the assembled company, and knew that Mr. Bowman was growing impatient for his dinner. His heart almost failed him now that the girl was out of sight. What if she should not prove to be accustomed to society, after all, and should show it? How embarrassing that would be! He had seen her only in a half-light as yet. How had he dared?

But it was too late now, for she was coming from the dressing-room, and Mrs. Bowman was approaching them with outstretched hands, and a welcome in her face.

"My dear Miss Remington, it is so good of you to help me out! I can see by the first glance that it is going to be a privilege to know you. I can't thank you enough for waiving formalities."

"It was very lovely of you to ask me," said the girl, with perfect composure, "a stranger——"

"Don't speak of it, my dear. Mr. Dunham's friends are not strangers, I assure you. Tryon, didn't you tell her how long we have known each other? I shall feel quite hurt if you have never mentioned me to her. Now, come, for my cook is in the last stages of despair over the dinner. Miss Remington, how do you manage to look so fresh and lovely after a long sea voyage? You must tell me your secret."

The young man looked down at the girl and saw that her dress was in perfect taste for the occasion, and also that she was very young and beautiful. He was watching her with a kind of proprietary pride as she moved forward to be introduced to the other guests, when he saw her sweep one quick glance about the room, and for just an instant hesitate and draw back. Her face grew white; then, with a supreme effort, she controlled her feelings, and went through her part with perfect ease.

When Judge Blackwell was introduced to the girl, he looked at her with what seemed to Dunham to be more than a passing interest; but the keen eyes were almost immediately transferred to his own face, and the young man had no further time to watch his protégé, as dinner was immediately announced.

Miss Remington was seated next to Dunham at the table, with the Judge on her other side. The young man was pleased with the arrangement, and sat furtively studying the delicate tinting of her face, the dainty line of cheek and chin and ear, the sweep of her dark lashes, and the ripple of her brown hair, as he tried to converse easily with her, as an old friend might.

At length the Judge turned to the girl and said:

"Miss Remington, you remind me strongly of a young woman who was in my office this afternoon."

The delicate color flickered out of the girl's face entirely, leaving even her lips white, but she lifted her dark eyes bravely to the kindly blue ones, and with sweet dignity baffled the questioned recognition in his look.

"Yes, you are so much like her that I would think you were—her sister perhaps, if it were not for the name," Judge Blackwell went on. "She was a most interesting and beautiful young lady." The old gentleman bestowed upon the girl a look that was like a benediction. "Excuse me for speaking of it, but her dress was something soft and beautiful, like yours, and seemed to suit her face. I was deeply interested in her, although until this afternoon she was a stranger. She came to me for a small matter of business, and after it was attended to, and before she received the papers, she disappeared! She had removed her hat and gloves, as she was obliged to wait some time for certain matters to be looked up, and these she left behind her. The hat is covered with long, handsome plumes of the color of rich cream in coffee."

Young Dunham glanced down at the cloth of the girl's gown, and was startled to find the same rich creamy-coffee tint in its silky folds; yet she did not show by so much as a flicker of an eyelash that she was passing under the keenest inspection. She toyed with the salted almonds beside her plate and held the heavy silver fork as firmly as if she were talking about the discovery of the north pole. Her voice was steady and natural as she asked, "How could she disappear?"

"Well, that is more than I can understand. There were three doors in the room where she sat, one opening into the inner office where I was at work, and two opening into a hall, one on the side and the other on the end opposite the freight elevator. We searched the entire building without finding a clew, and I am deeply troubled."

"Why should she want to disappear?" The question was asked coolly and with as much interest as a stranger would be likely to show.

"I cannot imagine," said the old man speculatively. "She apparently had health and happiness, if one may judge from her appearance, and she came to me of her own free will on a matter of business. Immediately after her disappearance, two well-dressed men entered my office and inquired for her. One had an intellectual head, but looked hard and cruel; the other was very handsome—and disagreeable. When he could not find the young lady, he laid claim to her hat, but I had it locked away. How could I know that man was her friend or her relative? I intend to keep that hat until the young woman herself claims it. I have not had anything happen that has so upset me in years."

"You don't think any harm has come to her?" questioned the girl.

"I cannot think what harm could, and yet—it is very strange. She was about the age of my dear daughter when she died, and I cannot get her out of my mind. When you first appeared in the doorway you gave me quite a start. I thought you were she. If I can find any trace of her, I mean to investigate this matter. I have a feeling that that girl needs a friend."

"I am sure she would be very happy to have a friend like you," said the girl, and there was something in the eyes that were raised to his that made the Judge's heart glow with admiration.

"Thank you," said he warmly. "That is most kind of you. But perhaps she has found a better friend by this time. I hope so."

"Or one as kind," she suggested in a low voice.

The conversation then became general, and the girl did not look up for several seconds; but the young man on her right, who had not missed a word of the previous tête-à-tête, could not give attention to the story Mrs. Blackwell was telling, for pondering what he had heard.

The ladies now left the table, and though this were the time that Dunham had counted upon for an acquaintance with the great judge who might hold a future career in his power, he could not but wish that he might follow them to the other room. He felt entire confidence in his new friend's ability to play her part to the end, but he wanted to watch her, to study her and understand her, if perchance he might solve the mystery that was ever growing more intense about her.

As she left the room, his eyes followed her. His hostess, in passing behind his chair, had whispered:

"I don't wonder you feel so about her. She is lovely. But please don't begrudge her to us for a few minutes. I promise you that you shall have your innings afterwards."

Then, without any warning and utterly against his will, this young man of much experience and self-control blushed furiously, and was glad enough when the door closed behind Mrs. Bowman.

Miss Remington walked into the drawing-room with a steady step, but with a rapidly beating heart. Her real ordeal had now come. She cast about in her mind for subjects of conversation which should forestall unsafe topics, and intuitively sought the protection of the Judge's wife. But immediately she saw her hostess making straight for the little Chippendale chair beside her.

"My dear, it is too lovely," she began. "So opportune! Do tell me how long you have known Tryon?"

The girl caught her breath and gathered her wits together. She looked up shyly into the pleasantly curious eyes of Mrs. Bowman, and a faint gleam of mischief came into her face.

"Why——" Her hesitation seemed only natural, and Mrs. Bowman decided that there must be something very special between these two. "Why, not so very long, Mrs. Bowman—not as long as you have known him." She finished with a smile which Mrs. Bowman decided was charming.

"Oh, you sly child!" she exclaimed, playfully tapping the round cheek with her fan. "Did you meet him when he was abroad this summer?"

"Oh, no, indeed!" said the girl, laughing now in spite of herself. "Oh, no; it was after his return."

"Then it must have been in the Adirondacks," went on the determined interlocutor. "Were you at——" But the girl interrupted her. She could not afford to discuss the Adirondacks, and the sight of the grand piano across the room had given her an idea.

"Mr. Dunham told me that you would like me to play something for you, as your musician friend has failed you. I shall be very glad to, if it will help you any. What do you care for? Something serious or something gay? Are you fond of Chopin, or Beethoven, or something more modern?"

Scenting a possible musical prodigy, and desiring most earnestly to give her guests a treat, Mrs. Bowman exclaimed in enthusiasm:

"Oh, how lovely of you! I hardly dared to ask, as Tryon was uncertain whether you would be willing. Suppose you give us something serious now, and later, when the men come in, we'll have the gay music. Make your own choice, though I'm very fond of Chopin, of course."

Without another word, the girl moved quietly over to the piano and took her seat. For just a moment her fingers wandered caressingly over the keys, as if they were old friends and she were having an understanding with them, then she began a Chopin Nocturne. Her touch was firm and velvety, and she brought out a bell-like tone from the instrument that made the little company of women realize that the player was mistress of her art. Her graceful figure and lovely head, with its simple ripples and waves of hair, were more noticeable than ever as she sat there, controlling the exquisite harmonies. Even Mrs. Blackwell stopped fanning and looked interested. Then she whispered to Mrs. Bowman: "A very sweet, young girl. That's a pretty piece she's playing." Mrs. Blackwell was sweet and commonplace and old-fashioned.

Mrs. Parker Bowman sat up with a pink glow in her cheeks and a light in her eyes. She began to plan how she might keep this acquisition and exploit her among her friends. It was her delight to bring out new features in her entertainments.

"We shall simply keep you playing until you drop from weariness," she announced ecstatically, when the last wailing, sobbing, soothing chord had died away; and the other ladies murmured, "How delightful!" and whispered their approval.

The girl smiled and rippled into a Chopin Valse, under cover of which those who cared to could talk in low tones. Afterwards the musician dashed into the brilliant movement of a Beethoven Sonata.

It was just as she was beginning Rubinstein's exquisite tone portrait, Kamennoi-Ostrow, that the gentlemen came in.

Tryon Dunham had had his much desired talk with the famous judge, but it had not been about law.

They had been drawn together by mutual consent, each discovering that the other was watching the young stranger as she left the dining-room.

"She is charming," said the old man, smiling into the face of the younger. "Is she an intimate friend?"

"I—I hope so," stammered Dunham. "That is, I should like to have her consider me so."

"Ah!" said the old man, looking deep into the other's eyes with a kindly smile, as if he were recalling pleasant experiences of his own. "You are a fortunate fellow. I hope you may succeed in making her think so. Do you know, she interests me more than most women, and in some way I cannot disconnect her with an occurrence which happened in my office this afternoon."

The young man showed a deep interest in the matter, and the Judge told the story again, this time more in detail.

They drew a little apart from the rest of the men. The host, who had been warned by his wife to give young Dunham an opportunity to talk with the Judge, saw that her plans were succeeding admirably.

When the music began in the other room the Judge paused a moment to listen, and then went on with his story.

"There is a freight elevator just opposite that left door of my office, and somehow I cannot but think it had something to do with the girl's disappearance, although the door was closed and the elevator was down on the cellar floor all the time, as nearly as I can find out."

The young man asked eager questions, feeling in his heart that the story might in some way explain the mystery of the young woman in the other room.

"Suppose you stop in the office to-morrow," said the Judge. "Perhaps you'll get a glimpse of her, and then bear me out in the statement that she's like your friend. By the way, who is making such exquisite music? Suppose we go and investigate. Mr. Bowman, will you excuse us if we follow the ladies? We are anxious to hear the music at closer range."

The other men rose and followed.

The girl did not pause or look up as they came in, but played on, while the company listened with the most rapt and wondering look. She was playing with an *empressement* which could not fail to command attention.

Tryon Dunham, standing just behind the Judge, was transfixed with amazement. That this delicate girl could bring forth such an entrancing volume of sound from the instrument was a great surprise. That she was so exquisite an artist filled him with a kind of intoxicating elation—it was as though she belonged to him.

At last she played Liszt's brilliant Hungarian Rhapsody, her slender hands taking the tremendous chords and octave runs with a precision and rapidity that seemed inspired. The final crash came in a shower of liquid jewels of sound, and then she turned to look at him, her one friend in that company of strangers.

He could see that she had been playing under a heavy strain. Her face looked weary and flushed, and her eyes were brilliant with feverish excitement. Those eyes seemed to be pleading with him now to set her free from the kindly scrutiny of those good-hearted, curious strangers. They gathered about her in delight, pouring their questions and praises upon her.

"Where did you study? With some great master, I am sure. Tell us all about yourself. We are dying to know, and will sit at your feet with great delight while you discourse."

Tryon Dunham interrupted these disquieting questions, by drawing his watch from his pocket with apparent hasty remembrance, and giving a well feigned exclamation of dismay.

"I'm sorry, Mrs. Bowman; it is too bad to interrupt this delightful evening," he apologized; "but I'm afraid if Miss

Remington feels that she must take the next train, we shall have to make all possible speed. Miss Remington, can you get your wraps on in three minutes? Our carriage is probably at the door now."

With a look of relief, yet keeping up her part of dismay over the lateness of the hour, the girl sprang to her feet, and hurried away to get her wraps, in spite of her protesting hostess. Mrs. Bowman was held at bay with sweet expressions of gratitude for the pleasant entertainment. The great black picture hat was settled becomingly on the small head, the black cloak thrown over her gown, and the gloves fitted on hurriedly to hide the fact that they were too large.

"And whom did you say you studied with?" asked the keen hostess, determined to be able to tell how great a guest she had harbored for the evening.

"Oh, is Mr. Dunham calling me, Mrs. Bowman? You will excuse me for hurrying off, won't you? And it has been so lovely of you to ask me—perfectly delightful to find friends this way when I was a stranger."

She hurried toward the stairway and down the broad steps, and the hostess had no choice but to follow her.

The other guests crowded out into the hall to bid them good-by and to tell the girl how much they had enjoyed the music. Mrs. Blackwell insisted upon kissing the smooth cheek of the young musician, and whispered in her ear: "You play very nicely, my dear. I should like to hear you again some time." The kindness in her tone almost brought a rush of tears to the eyes of the weary, anxious girl.

3

DUNHAM hurried her off amid the good-byes of the company, and in a moment more they were shut into the semi-darkness of the four-wheeler and whirled from the too hospitable door.

As soon as the door was shut, the girl began to tremble.

"Oh, we ought not to have done that!" she exclaimed with a shiver of recollection. "They were so very kind. It was dreadful to impose upon them. But—you were not to blame. It was my fault. It was very kind of you."

"We did not impose upon them!" he exclaimed peremptorily. "You are my friend, and that was all that we claimed. For the rest, you have certainly made good. Your wonderful music! How I wish I might hear more of it some time!"

The carriage paused to let a trolley pass, and a strong arc-light beat in upon the two. A passing stranger peered curiously at them, and the girl shrank back in fear. It was momentary, but the minds of the two were brought back to the immediate necessities of the occasion.

"Now, what may I do for you?" asked Dunham in a

quiet, business-like tone, as if it were his privilege and right to do all that was to be done. "Have you thought where you would like to go?"

"I have not been able to do much thinking. It required all my wits to act with the present. But I know that I must not be any further trouble to you. You have done more already than any one could expect. If you can have the carriage stop in some quiet, out-of-the-way street where I shall not be noticed, I will get out and relieve you. If I hadn't been so frightened at first, I should have had more sense than to burden you this way. I hope some day I shall be able to repay your kindness, though I fear it is too great ever to repay."

"Please don't talk in that way," said he protestingly. "It has been a pleasure to do the little that I have done, and you have more than repaid it by the delight you have given me and my friends. I could not think of leaving you until you are out of your trouble, and if you will only give me a little hint of how to help, I will do my utmost for you. Are you quite sure you were followed? Don't you think you could trust me enough to tell me a little more about the matter?"

She shuddered visibly.

"Forgive me," he murmured. "I see it distresses you. Of course it is unpleasant to confide in an utter stranger. I will not ask you to tell me. I will try to think for you. Suppose we go to the station and get you a ticket to somewhere. Have you any preference? You can trust me not to tell any one where you have gone, can you not?" There was a kind of rebuke in his tone, and her eyes, as she lifted them to his face, were full of tears.

"Oh, I do trust you!" she cried, distressed. "You must not think that, but—you do not understand."

"Forgive me," he said again, holding out his hand in appeal. She laid her little gloved hand in his for an instant.

"You are so kind!" she murmured, as if it were the only

thing she could think of. Then she added suddenly:

"But I cannot buy a ticket. I have no money with me, and I—"

"Don't think of that for an instant. I will gladly supply your need. A little loan should not distress you."

"But I do not know when I shall be able to repay it," she faltered, "unless"—she hastily drew off her glove and slipped a glittering ring from her finger—"unless you will let this pay for it. I do not like to trouble you so, but the stone is worth a good deal."

"Indeed," he protested, "I couldn't think of taking your ring. Let me do this. It is such a small thing. I shall never miss it. Let it rest until you are out of your trouble, at least."

"Please!" she insisted, holding out the ring. "I shall get right out of this carriage unless you do."

"But perhaps some one gave you the ring, and you are attached to it."

"My father," she answered briefly, "and he would want me to use it this way." She pressed the ring into his hand almost impatiently.

His fingers closed over the jewel impulsively. Somehow, it thrilled him to hold the little thing, yet warm from her fingers. He had forgotten that she was a stranger. His mind was filled with the thought of how best to help her.

"I will keep it until you want it again," he said kindly.

"You need not do that, for I shall not claim it," she declared. "You are at liberty to sell it. I know it is worth a good deal."

"I shall certainly keep it until I am sure you do not want it yourself," he repeated. "Now let us talk about this journey of yours. We are almost at the station. Have you any preference as to where you go? Have you friends to whom you could go?"

She shook her head.

"There are trains to New York every hour almost."

"Oh, no!" she gasped in a frightened tone.

"And to Washington often."

"I should rather not go to Washington," she breathed again.

"Pittsburgh, Chicago?" he hazarded.

"Chicago will do," she asserted with relief. Then the carriage stopped before the great station, ablaze with light and throbbing with life. Policemen strolled about, and trolley-cars twinkled in every direction. The girl shrank back into the shadows of the carriage for an instant, as if she feared to come out from the sheltering darkness. Her escort half defined her hesitation.

"Don't feel nervous," he said in a low tone. "I will see that no one harms you. Just walk into the station as if you were my friend. You are, you know, a friend of long standing, for we have been to a dinner together. I might be escorting you home from a concert. No one will notice us. Besides, that hat and coat are disguise enough."

He hurried her through the station and up to the ladies' waiting-room, where he found a quiet corner and a large rocking-chair, in which he placed her so that she might look out of the great window upon the panorama of the evening street, and yet be thoroughly screened from all intruding glances by the big leather and brass screen of the "ladies' boot-black."

He was gone fifteen minutes, during which the girl sat quietly in her chair, yet alert, every nerve strained. At any moment the mass of faces she was watching might reveal one whom she dreaded to see, or a detective might place his hand upon her shoulder with a quiet "Come with me."

When Dunham came back, the nervous start she gave showed him how tense and anxious had been her mind. He studied her lovely face under the great hat, and noted the dark shadows beneath her eyes. He felt that he must do something to relieve her. It was unbearable to him that this young girl should be adrift, friendless, and apparently a victim to some terrible fear.

Drawing up a chair beside her, he began talking about her ticket.

"You must remember I was utterly at your mercy," she smiled sadly. "I simply had to let you help me."

"I should be glad to pay double for the pleasure you have given me in allowing me to help you," he said.

Just at that moment a boy in blue uniform planted a sole-leather suit-case at his feet, and exclaimed: "Here you are, Mr. Dunham. Had a fierce time findin' you. Thought you said you would be by the elevator door."

"So I did," confessed the young man. "I didn't think you had time to get down yet. Well, you found me anyhow, Harkness."

The boy took the silver given him, touched his hat, and sauntered off.

"You see," explained Dunham, "it wasn't exactly the thing for you to be travelling without a bit of baggage. I thought it might help them to trace you if you really were being followed. So I took the liberty of 'phoning over to the club-house and telling the boy to bring down the suit-case that I left there yesterday. I don't exactly know what's in it. I had the man pack it and send it down to me, thinking I might stay all night at the club. Then I went home, after all, and forgot to take it along. It probably hasn't anything very appropriate for a lady's costume, but there may be a hair-brush and some soap and handkerchiefs. And, anyhow, if you'll accept it, it'll be something for you to hitch on to. One feels a little lost even for one night without a rag one can call one's own except a Pullman towel. I thought it might give you the appearance of a regular traveller, you know, and not a runaway."

He tried to make her laugh about it, but her face was deeply serious as she looked up at him.

"I think this is the kindest and most thoughtful thing

you have done yet," she said. "I don't see how I can ever, ever thank you!"

"Don't try," he returned gaily. "There's your train being called. We'd better go right out and make you comfortable. You are beginning to be very tired."

She did not deny it, but rose to follow him, scanning the waiting-room with one quick, frightened look. An obsequious porter at the gate seized the suit-case and led them in state to the Pullman.

The girl found herself established in the little drawing-room compartment, and her eyes gave him thanks again. She knew the seclusion and the opportunity to lock the compartment door would give her relief from the constant fear that an unwelcome face might at any moment appear beside her.

"The conductor on this train is an old acquaintance of mine," he explained as that official came through the car. "I have taken this trip with him a number of times. Just sit down a minute. I am going to ask him to look out for you and see that no one annoys you."

The burly official looked grimly over his glasses at the sweet face under the big black hat, while Tryon Dunham explained, "She's a friend of mine. I hope you'll be good to her." In answer, he nodded grim assent with a smileless alacrity which was nevertheless satisfactory and comforting. Then the young man walked through the train to interview the porter and the newsboy, and in every way to arrange for a pleasant journey for one who three hours before had been unknown to him. As he went, he reflected that he would rather enjoy being conductor himself just for that night. He felt a strange reluctance toward giving up the oversight of the young woman whose destiny for a few brief hours had been thrust upon him, and who was about to pass out of his world again.

When he returned to her he found the shades closely

drawn and the girl sitting in the sheltered corner of the section, where she could not be seen from the aisle, but where she could watch in the mirror the approach of any one. She welcomed him with a smile, but instantly urged him to leave the train, lest he be carried away.

He laughed at her fears, and told her there was plenty of time. Even after the train had given its preliminary shudder, he lingered to tell her that she must be sure to let him know by telegraph if she needed any further help; and at last swung himself from the platform after the train was in full motion.

Immediately he remembered that he had not given her any money. How could he have forgotten? And there was the North Side Station yet to be passed before she would be out of danger. Why had he not remained on the train until she was past that stop, and then returned on the next train from the little flag-station a few miles above, where he could have gotten the conductor to slow up for him? The swiftly moving cars asked the question as the long train flew by him. The last car was almost past when he made a daring dash and flung himself headlong upon the platform, to the horror of several trainmen who stood on the adjoining tracks.

"Gee!" said one, shaking his head. "What does that dude think he is made of, any way? Like to got his head busted that time, fer sure."

The brakeman, coming out of the car door with his lantern, dragged him to his feet, brushed him off, and scolded him vigorously. The young man hurried through the car, oblivious of the eloquent harangue, happy only to feel the floor jolting beneath his feet, and to know that he was safe on board.

He found the girl sitting where he had left her, only she had flung up the shade of the window next to her, and was gazing with wide, frightened eyes into the fast flying darkness. He touched her gently on the shoulder, and she turned with a cry.

"Oh, I thought you had fallen under the train!" she said in an awed voice. "It was going so fast! But you did not get off, after all, did you? Now, what can you do? It is too bad, and all on my account."

"Yes, I got off," he said doggedly, sitting down opposite her and pulling his tie straight. "I got off, but it wasn't altogether satisfactory, and so I got on again. There wasn't much time for getting on gracefully, but you'll have to excuse it. The fact is, I couldn't bear to leave you alone just yet. I couldn't rest until I knew you had passed the North Side Station. Besides, I had forgotten to give you any money."

"Oh, but you mustn't!" she protested, her eyes eloquent with feeling.

"Please don't say that," he went on eagerly. "I can get off later and take the down train, you know. Really, the fact is, I couldn't let you go right out of existence this way without knowing more about you."

"Oh!" she gasped, turning a little white about the lips, and drawing closer into her corner.

"Don't feel that way," he said. "I'm not going to bother you. You couldn't think that of me, surely. But isn't it only fair that you should show me a little consideration? Just give me an address, or something, where I could let you know if I heard of anything that concerned you. Of course it isn't likely I shall, but it seems to me you might at least let me know you are safe."

"I will promise you that," she said earnestly. "You know I'm going to send you back these things." She touched the cloak and the hat. "You might need them to keep you from having to explain their absence," she reminded him.

The moments fairly flew. They passed the North Side Station, and were nearing the flag station. After that there would be no more stops until past midnight. The young man knew he must get off.

"I have almost a mind to go on to Chicago and see that you are safely located," he said with sudden daring. "It seems too terrible to set you adrift in the world this way."

"Indeed, you must not," said the young woman, with a gentle dignity. "Have you stopped to think what people—what your mother, for instance—would think of me if she were ever to know I had permitted such a thing? You know you must not. Please don't speak of it again."

"I cannot help feeling that I ought to take care of you," he said, but half convinced.

"But I cannot permit it," she said firmly, lifting her trustful eyes to smile at him.

"Will you promise to let me know if you need anything?"

"No, I'm afraid I cannot promise even that," she answered, "because, while you have been a true friend to me, the immediate and awful necessity is, I hope, past."

"You will at least take this," he said, drawing from his pocket an inconspicuous purse of beautiful leather, and putting into it all the money his pockets contained. "I saw you had no pocketbook," he went on, "and I ventured to get this one in the drug-store below the station. Will you accept it from me? I have your ring, you know, and when you take the ring back you may, if you wish, return the purse. I wish it were a better one, but it was the most decent one they had. You will need it to carry your ticket. And I have put in the change. It would not do for you to be entirely without money. I'm sorry it isn't more. There are only nine dollars and seventy-five cents left. Do you think that will see you through? If there had been any place down-town here where I could cash a check at this time of night, I should have made it more."

He looked at her anxiously as he handed over the pocketbook. It seemed a ridiculously small sum with which to begin a journey alone, especially for a young woman of her apparent refinement. On the other hand, his friends would probably say he was a fool for having hazarded so much as he had upon an unknown woman, who was perhaps an adventuress. However, he had thrown discretion to the winds, and was undeniably interested in his new acquaintance.

"How thoughtful you are!" said the girl. "It would have been most embarrassing not to have a place to put my ticket, nor any money. This seems a fortune after being penniless"—she smiled ruefully. "Are you sure you have not reduced yourself to that condition? Have you saved enough to carry you home?"

"Oh, I have my mileage book with me," he said happily. It pleased him absurdly that she had not declined the pocketbook.

"Thank you so much. I shall return the price of the ticket and this money as soon as possible," said the girl earnestly.

"You must not think of that," he protested. "You know I have your ring. That is far more valuable than anything I have given you."

"Oh, but you said you were going to keep the ring, so that will not pay for this. I want to be sure that you lose nothing."

He suddenly became aware that the train was whistling, and that the conductor was motioning him to go.

"But you have not told me your name," he cried in dismay.

"You have named me," she answered, smiling. "I am Mary Remington."

"But that is not your real name."

"You may call me Mary if you like," she said "Now go, please, quick! I'm afraid you'll get hurt."

"You will remember that I am your friend?"

"Yes, thank you. Hurry, please!"

The train paused long enough for him to step in front of

her window and wave his hat in salute. Then she passed on into the night, and only two twinkling lights, like diminishing red berries, marked the progress of the train until it disappeared in the cut. Nothing was left but the hollow echoes of its going, which the hills gave back.

4

DUNHAM listened as long as his ear could catch the sound, then a strange desolation settled down upon him. How was it that a few short hours ago he had known nothing, cared nothing, about this stranger? And now her going had left things blank enough! It was foolish, of course—just highly wrought nerves over this most extraordinary occurrence. Life had heretofore run in such smooth, conventional grooves as to have been almost prosaic; and now to be suddenly plunged into romance and mystery unbalanced him for the time. To-morrow, probably, he would again be able to look sane living in the face, and perhaps call himself a fool for his most unusual interest in this chance acquaintance; but just at this moment when he had parted from her, when the memory of her lovely face and pure eyes lingered with him, when her bravery and fear were both so fresh in his mind, and the very sound of her music was still in his brain, he simply could not without a pang turn back again to life which contained no solution of her mystery, no hope of another vision of her face.

The little station behind him was closed, though a light over the desk shone brightly through its front window and the telegraph sounder was clicking busily. The operator had gone over the hill with an important telegram, leaving the station door locked. The platform was windy and cheerless, with a view of a murky swamp, and the sound of deep-throated inhabitants croaking out a late fall concert. A rusty-throated cricket in a crack of the platform wailed a plaintive note now and then, and off beyond the swamp, in the edge of the wood, a screech-owl hooted.

Turning impatiently from the darkness, Dunham sought the bright window, in front of which lay a newspaper. He could read the large headlines of a column—no more, for the paper was upside down, and a bunch of bill-heads lay partly across it. It read:

MYSTERIOUS DISAPPEARANCE OF YOUNG AND PRETTY WOMAN

His heart stood still, and then went thudding on in dull, horrid blows. Vainly he tried to read further. He followed every visible word of that paper to discover its date and origin, but those miserable bill-heads frustrated his effort. He felt like dashing his hand through the glass, but reflected that the act might result in his being locked up in some miserable country jail. He tried the window and gave the door another vicious shake, but all to no purpose. Finally he turned on his heel and walked up and down for an hour, tramping the length of the shaky platform, back and forth, till the train rumbled up. As he took his seat in the car he saw the belated agent come running up the platform with a lighted lantern on his arm, and a package of letters, which he handed to the brakeman, but there was not time to beg the newspaper from him. Dunham's indignant mind continued to dwell upon the headlines, to the annoying accompaniment of screech-owl and frog and cricket. He resented the adjective "pretty." Why should any reporter dare to apply that word to a sweet and lovely woman? It seemed so superficial, so belittling, and—but then, of course, this headline did not apply to his new friend. It was some other poor creature, some one to whom perhaps the word "pretty" really applied; some one who was not really beautiful, only pretty.

At the first stop a man in front got out, leaving a newspaper in the seat. With eager hands, Dunham leaned forward and grasped it, searching its columns in vain for the tantalizing headlines. But there were others equally arrestive. This paper announced the mysterious disappearance of a young actress who was suspecting of poisoning her husband. When seen last, she was boarding a train en route to Washington. She had not arrived, there, however, so far as could be discovered. It was supposed that she was lingering in the vicinity of Philadelphia or Baltimore. There were added a few incriminating details concerning her relationship with her dead husband, and a brief sketch of her sensational life. The paragraph closed with the statement that she was an accomplished musician.

The young man frowned and, opening his window, flung the scandalous sheet to the breeze. He determined to forget what he had read, yet the lines kept coming before his eyes.

When he reached the city he went to the news-stand in the station, where was an agent who knew him, and procured a copy of every paper on sale. Then, instead of hurrying home, he found a seat in a secluded corner and proceeded to examine his purchases.

In large letters on the front page of a New York paper blazed:

HOUSE ROBBED OF JEWELS WORTH
TEN THOUSAND DOLLARS BY BEAUTIFUL
YOUNG ADVENTURESS MASQUERADING
AS A PARLOR MAID

He ran his eye down the column and gathered that she was still at large, though the entire police force of New York was on her track. He shivered at the thought, and began to feel sympathy for all wrong-doers and truants from the law. It was horrible to have detectives out everywhere watching for beautiful young women, just when this one in whom his interest centred was trying to escape from something.

He turned to another paper, only to be met by the words:

ESCAPE OF FAIR LUNATIC

and underneath:

Prison walls could not confine Miss Nancy Lee, who last week threw a lighted lamp at her mother, setting fire to the house, and then attempted suicide. The young woman seems to have recovered her senses, and professes to know nothing of what happened, but the physicians say she is liable to another attack of insanity, and deem it safe to keep her confined. She escaped during the night, leaving no clew to her whereabouts. How she managed to get open the window through which she left the asylum is still a mystery.

In disgust he flung the paper from him and took up another.

FOUL PLAY SUSPECTED! BEAUTIFUL
YOUNG HEIRESS MISSING

His soul turned sick within him. He looked up and saw a little procession of late revellers rushing out to the last suburban train, the girls leaving a trail of orris perfume and a vision of dainty opera cloaks. One of the men was a city friend of his. Dunham half envied him his unperturbed mind. To be sure, he would not get back to the city till three in the morning, but he would have no visions of robberies and fair lunatics and hard pressed maidens unjustly pursued, to mar his rest.

Dunham buttoned his coat and turned up his collar as he started out into the street, for the night had turned cold, and his nerves made him chilly. As he walked, the blood began to race more healthily in his veins, and the horrors of the evening papers were dispelled. In their place came pleasant memories of the evening at Mrs. Bowman's, of the music, and of their ride and talk together. In his heart a hope began to rise that her dark days would pass, and that he might find her again and know her better.

His brief night's sleep was cut short by a sharp knock at his door the next morning. He awoke with a confused idea of being on a sleeping-car, and wondered if he had plenty of time to dress, but his sister's voice quickly dispelled the illusion.

"Tryon, aren't you almost ready to come down to breakfast? Do hurry, please. I've something awfully important to consult you about."

His sister's tone told him there was need for haste if he would keep in her good graces, so he made a hurried toilet and went down, to find his household in a state of subdued excitement.

"I'm just as worried as I can be," declared his mother. "I want to consult you, Tryon. I have put such implicit confidence in Norah, and I cannot bear to accuse her unjustly, but I have missed a number of little things lately. There was my gold link bag—"

"Mother, you know you said you were sure you left that at the Century Club."

"Don't interrupt, Cornelia. Of course it is possible I left it at the club rooms, but I begin to think now that I didn't have it with me at all. Then there is my opal ring. To be sure, it isn't worth a great deal, but one who will take little things will take large ones."

"What's the matter, Mother? Norah been appropriating property not her own?"

"I'm very much afraid she has, Tryon. What would you do about it? It is so unpleasant to charge a person with stealing. It is such a vulgar thing to steal. Somehow I thought Nora was more refined."

"Why, I suppose there's nothing to do but just charge her with it, is there? Are you quite sure it is gone? What is it, any way? A ring, did you say?"

"No, it's a hat," said Cornelia shortly. "A sixty-dollar hat. I wish I'd kept it now, and then she wouldn't have dared. It had two beautiful willow ostrich plumes on it, but mother didn't think it was becoming. She wanted some color about it instead of all black. I left it in my room, and charged Norah to see that the man got it when he called, and now the man comes and says he wants the hat, and it is *gone!* Norah insists that when she last saw it, it was in my room. But of course that's absurd, for there was nobody else to take it but Thompson, and he's been in the family for so long."

"Nonsense!" said her brother sharply, dropping his fruit knife in his plate with a rattle that made the young woman jump. "Cornelia, I'm ashamed of you, thinking that poor, innocent girl has stolen your hat. Why, she wouldn't steal a pin, I am sure. You can tell she's honest by looking into her eyes. Girls with blue eyes like that don't lie and steal."

"Really!" Cornelia remarked haughtily. "You seem to know a great deal about her eyes. You may feel differently when I find the hat in her possession."

"Cornelia," interrupted Tryon, quite beside himself, "don't think of such a thing as speaking to that poor girl about that hat. I know she hasn't stolen it. The hat will probably be found, and then how will you feel?"

"But I tell you the hat cannot be found!" said the exasperated sister. "And I shall just have to pay for a hat that I can never wear."

"Mother, I appeal to you," said the son earnestly. "Don't allow Cornelia to speak of the hat to the girl. I wouldn't have such an injustice done in our house. The hat will turn up soon if you just go about the matter calmly. You'll find it quite naturally and unexpectedly, perhaps. Any way, if you don't, I'll pay for the hat, rather than have the girl suspected."

"But, Tryon," protested his mother, "if she isn't honest, you know we wouldn't want her about."

"Honest, Mother? She's as honest as the day is long. I am certain of that."

The mother rose reluctantly.

"Well, we might let it go another day," she consented. Then, looking up at the sky, she added, "I wonder if it is going to rain. I have a Reciprocity meeting on for to-day, and I'm a delegate to some little unheard-of place. It usually does rain when one goes into the country, I've noticed."

She went into the hall, and presently returned with a distressed look upon her face.

"Tryon, I'm afraid you're wrong," she said. "Now my rain-coat is missing. My new rain-coat! I hung it up in the hall-closet with my own hands, after it came from the store. I really think something ought to be done!"

"There! I hope you see!" said Cornelia severely. "I think it's high time something was done. I shall 'phone for a detective at once!"

"Cornelia, you'll do nothing of the kind," her brother protested, now thoroughly aroused. "I'll agree to pay for the hat and the rain-coat if they are not forthcoming before a fortnight passes, but you simply shall not ruin that poor girl's reputation. I insist, Mother, that you put a stop to such rash proceedings. I'll make myself personally responsible for that girl's honesty."

"Well, of course, Tryon, if you wish it—" said his mother, with anxious hesitation.

"I certainly do wish it, Mother. I shall take it as personal if anything is done in this matter without consulting me. Remember, Cornelia, I will not have any trifling. A girl's reputation is certainly worth more than several hats and rain-coats, and I *know* she has not taken them."

He walked from the dining-room and from the house in angry dignity, to the astonishment of his mother and sister, to whom he was usually courtesy itself. Consulting him about household matters was as a rule merely a form, for he almost never interfered. The two women looked at each other in startled bewilderment.

"Mother," said Cornelia, "you don't suppose he can have fallen in love with Norah, do you? Why, she's Irish and freckled! And Tryon has always been so fastidious!"

"Cornelia! How dare you suggest such a thing? Tryon is a *Dunham*. Whatever else a Dunham may or may not do, he never does anything low or unrefined."

The small, prim, stylish mother looked quite regal in her aristocratic rage.

"But, Mother, one reads such dreadful things in the papers now. Of course Tryon would never *marry* any one like that, but—"

"Cornelia!"—her mother's voice had almost reached a patrician scream—"I forbid you to mention the subject again. I cannot think where you learned to voice such thoughts."

"Well, my goodness, Mother, I don't mean anything, only I do wish I had my hat. I always did like all black. I can't imagine what ails Try, if it isn't that."

Tryon Dunham took his way to his office much perturbed in mind. Perplexities seemed to be thickening about him. With the dawn of the morning had come that sterner common-sense which told him he was a fool for having taken up with a strange young woman on the street, who was so evidently flying from justice. He had deceived not only his intimate friends by palming her off as a fit companion for them, but his mother and sister. He had practically stolen their garments, and had squandered more than fifty dollars of his own money. And what had he to show for all this? The memory of a sweet face, the lingering beauty of the name "Mary" when she bade him good-by, and a diamond ring. The cool morning light presented the view that the ring was probably valueless, and that he was a fool.

Ah, the ring! A sudden warm thrill shot through him, and his hand searched his vest pocket, where he had hastily put the jewel before leaving his room. That was something tangible. He could at least know what it was worth, and so make sure once for all whether he had been deceived. No, that would not be fair either, for her father might have made her think it was valuable, or he might even have been taken in himself, if he were not a judge of jewels.

Dunham examined it as he walked down the street, too perplexed with his own tumultuous thoughts to remember his usual trolley. He slipped the ring on his finger and let it catch the morning sunlight, now shining broad and clear in spite of the hovering rain-clouds in the distance. And gloriously did the sun illumine the diamond, burrowing into the great depths of its clear white heart, and causing it to break into a million fires of glory, flashing and glancing until it fairly dazzled him. The stone seemed to be of unusual beauty and purity, but he would step into the diamond shop as he passed and make sure. He had a friend there who could tell him all about it. His step quickened, and he covered the distance in a short time.

After the morning greeting, he handed over his ring.

"This belongs to a friend of mine," he said, trying to look unconcerned. "I should like to know if the stone is genuine, and about what it is worth."

His friend took the ring and retired behind a curious little instrument for the eye, presently emerging with a respectful look upon his face.

"Your friend is fortunate to have such a beautiful stone. It is unusually clear and white, and exquisitely cut. I should say it was worth at least"—he paused and then named a sum which startled Dunham, even accustomed as he was to counting values in high figures. He took the jewel back with a kind of awe. Where had this mysterious lady acquired this wondrous bauble which she had tossed to him for a trifle? In a tumult of feeling, he went on to his office more perplexed than ever. Suspicions of all sorts crowded thickly into his mind, but for every thought that shadowed the fair reputation of the lady, there came into his mind her clear eyes and cast out all doubts. Finally, after a bad hour of trying to work, he slipped the ring on his little finger, determined to wear it and thus prove to himself his belief in her, at least until he had absolute proof against her. Then he took up his hat and went out, deciding to accept Judge Blackwell's invitation to visit his office. He found a cordial reception, and the Judge talked business in a most satisfactory manner. His proposals bade fair to bring about some of the dearest wishes of the young man's heart, and yet as he left the building he was thinking more about the mysterious stranger who had disappeared from the Judge's office the day before than about the wonderful good luck that had come to him in a business way.

They had not talked much about her. The Judge had brought out her hat—a beautiful velvet one, with exquisite plumes—her gloves, a costly leather purse, and a fine hemstitched handkerchief, and as he put them sadly away on a closet shelf, he said no trace of her had as yet been found.

On his way toward his own office, Tryon Dunham pondered the remarkable coincidence which had made him the possessor of two parts of the same mystery—for he had no doubt that the hat belonged to the young woman who had claimed his help the evening before.

Meantime, the girl who was speeding along toward Chicago had not forgotten him. She could not if she would, for all about her were reminders of him. The conductor took charge of her ticket, telling her in his gruff, kind way what time they would arrive in the city. The porter was solicitous about her comfort, the newsboy brought the latest magazines and a box of chocolates and laid them at her shrine with a smile of admiration and the words, "Th' g'n'lmun sent 'em!" The suitcase lay on the seat opposite, the reflection of her face in the window-glass, as she gazed into the inky darkness outside, was crowned by the hat he had provided, and when she moved the silken rustle of the rain-coat reminded her of his kindness and forethought. She put her head back and closed her eyes, and for just an instant let her weary, over-wrought mind think what it would mean if the man from whom she was fleeing had been such as this one seemed to be.

By and by, she opened the suit-case, half doubtfully, feeling that she was almost intruding upon another's possessions.

There were a dress-suit and a change of fine linen, handkerchiefs, neckties, a pair of gloves, a soft, black felt negligee hat folded, a large black silk muffler, a bath-robe, and the usual silver-mounted brushes, combs, and other toilet articles. She looked them over in a business-like way, trying to see how she could make use of them. Removing her hat, she covered it with the silk muffler, to protect it from dust. Then she took off her dress and wrapped herself in the soft bath-robe, wondering as she did so at her willingness to put on a stranger's garments. Somehow, in her brief acquaintance with this man, he had impressed her with his own pleasant fastidiousness, so that there was a kind of pleasure in using his things, as if they had been those of a valued friend.

She touched the electric button that controlled the lights in the little apartment, and lay down in the darkness to think out her problem of the new life that lay before her.

BEGINNING with the awful moment when she first realized her danger and the necessity for immediate flight, she lived over every perilous instant, her nerves straining, her breath bated as if she were experiencing it all once more. The horror of it! Her own hopeless, helpless condition! But finally, because her trouble was new and her body and mind, though worn with excitement, were healthy and young, she sank into a deep sleep, without having decided at all what she should do.

At last she woke from a terrible dream, in which the hand of her pursuer was upon her, and her preserver was in the dark distance. With that strange insistence which torments the victim of such dreams, she was obliged to lie still and imagine it out, again and again, until the face and voice of the young man grew very real in the darkness, and she longed inexpressibly for the comfort of his presence once more.

At length she shook off these pursuing thoughts and deliberately roused herself to plan her future.

The first necessity, she decided, was to change her appearance so far as possible, so that if news of her escape, with full description, had been telegraphed, she might evade notice. To that end, she arose in the early dawning of a gray and misty morning, and arranged her hair as she had never worn it before, in two braids and wound closely about her head. It was neat, and appropriate to the vocation which she had decided upon, and it made more difference in her appearance than any other thing she could have done. All the soft, fluffy fulness of rippling hair that had framed her face was drawn close to her head, and the smooth bands gave her the simplicity and severity of a saint in some old picture. She pinned up her gown until it did not show below the long black coat, and folded a white linen handkerchief about her throat over the delicate lace and garniture of the modish waist. Then she looked dubiously at the hat.

With a girl's instinct, her first thought was for her borrowed plumage. A fine mist was slanting down and had fretted the window-pane until there was nothing visible but dull gray shadows of a world that flew monotonously by. With sudden remembrance, she opened the suit-case and took out the folded black hat, shook it into shape, and put it on. It was mannish, of course, but girls often wore such hats.

As she surveyed herself in the long mirror of her door, the slow color stole into her cheeks. Yet the costume was not unbecoming, nor unusual. She looked like a simple school-girl, or a young business woman going to her day's work.

But she looked at the fashionable proportions of the other hat with something like alarm. How could she protect it? She did not for a moment think of abandoning it, for it was her earnest desire to return it at once, unharmed, to its kind purloiner.

She summoned the newsboy and purchased three thick newspapers. From these, with the aid of a few pins, she made a large package of the hat. To be sure, it did not look like a hat when it was done, but that was all the better. The feathers were upheld and packed softly about with bits of paper crushed together to make a springy cushion, and the whole built out and then covered over with paper. She reflected that girls who wore their hair wound about their heads and covered by plain felt hats would not be unlikely to carry large newspaper-wrapped packages through the city streets.

She decided to go barehanded, and put the white kid gloves in the suit-case, but she took off her beautiful rings, and hid them safely inside her dress.

When the porter came to announce that her breakfast was waiting in the dining-car, he looked at her almost with a start, but she answered his look with a pleasant, "Good morning. You see I'm fixed for a damp day."

"Yes, miss," said the man deferentially. "It's a nasty day outside. I 'spect Chicago'll be mighty wet. De wind's off de lake, and de rain's comin' from all way 'twoncet."

She sacrificed one of her precious quarters to get rid of the attentive porter, and started off with a brisk step down the long platform to the station. It was part of her plan to get out of the neighborhood as quickly as possible, so she followed the stream of people who instead of going into the waiting-room veered off to the street door and out into the great, wet, noisy world. With the same reasoning, she followed a group of people into a car, which presently brought her into the neighborhood of the large stores, as she had hoped it would. It was with relief that she recognized the name on one of the stores as being of world-wide reputation.

Well for her that she was an experienced shopper. She went straight to the millinery department and arranged to have the hat boxed and sent to the address Dunham had given her. Her gentle voice and handsome raincoat proclaimed her a lady and commanded deference and respectful attention. As she walked away, she had an odd feeling of having communicated with her one friend and preserver.

It had cost less to express the hat than she had feared, yet her stock of money was woefully small. Some kind of a dress she must have, and a wrap, that she might be disguised, but what could she buy and yet have something left for food? There was no telling how long it would be before she could replenish her purse. Life must be reduced to its lowest terms. True, she had jewelry which might be sold, but that would scarcely be safe, for if she were watched, she might easily be identified by it. What did the very poor do, who were yet respectable?

The ready-made coats and skirts were entirely beyond her means, even those that had been marked down. With a hopeless feeling, she walked aimlessly down between the tables of goods. The suit-case weighed like lead, and she put it on the floor to rest her aching arms. Lifting her eyes, she saw a sign over a table:

Linene Skirts, 75 cts. and $1.00

Here was a ray of hope. She turned eagerly to examine them. Piles of sombre skirts, blue and black and tan. They were stout and coarse and scant, and not of the latest cut, but what mattered it? She decided on a seventy-five cent black one. It seemed pitiful to have to economize in a matter of twenty-five cents, when she had been used to counting her money by dollars, yet there was a feeling of exultation at having gotten for that price any skirt at all that would do. A dim memory of what she had read about ten-cent lodging-houses, where human beings were herded like cattle, hovered over her.

Growing wise with experience, she discovered that she could get a black sateen shirt-waist for fifty cents. Rubbers and a cotton umbrella took another dollar and a half. She must save at least a dollar to send back the suit-case by express.

A bargain-table of odds and ends of woollen jackets, golf vests, and old fashioned blouse sweaters, selling off at a dollar apiece, solved the problem of a wrap. She selected a dark blouse, of an ugly, purply blue, but thick and warm. Then with her precious packages she asked a pleasant-faced saleswoman if there were any place near where she could slip on a walking skirt she had just bought to save her other skirt from the muddy streets. She was ushered into a little fitting-room near by. It was only about four feet square, with one chair and a tiny table, but it looked like a palace to the girl in her need, and as she fastened the door and looked at the bare painted walls that reached but a foot or so above her head and had no ceiling, she wished with all her heart that such a refuge as this might be her own somewhere in the great, wide, fearful world.

Rapidly she slipped off her fine, silk-lined cloth garments, and put on the stiff sateen waist and the coarse black skirt. Then she surveyed herself, and was not ill pleased. There was a striking lack of collar and belt. She sought out a black necktie and pinned it about her waist, and then, with a protesting frown, she deliberately tore a strip from the edge of one of the fine hem-stitched handkerchiefs, and folded it in about her neck in a turn-over collar. The result was quite startling and unfamiliar. The gown, the hair, the hat, and the neat collar gave her the look of a young nurse-girl or upper servant. On the whole, the disguise could not have been better. She added the blue woollen blouse, and felt certain that even her most intimate friends would not recognize her. She folded the rain-coat, and placed it smoothly in the suit-case, then with dismay remembered that she had nothing in which to put her own cloth dress, save the few inadequate paper wrappings that had come about her simple purchases. Vainly she tried to reduce the dress to a bundle that would be covered by the papers. It was of no use. She looked down at the suit-case. There was room for the dress in there, but she wanted to send Mr. Dunham's property back at once. She might leave the dress in the store, but some detective with an accurate description of that dress might be watching, find it, and trace her. Besides, she shrank from leaving her garments about in public places. If there had been any bridge near at hand where she might unobserved throw the dress into a dark river, or a consuming fire where she might dispose of it, she would have done it. But whatever she was to do with it must be done at once. Her destiny must be settled before the darkness came down. She folded the dress smoothly and laid it in the suit-case, under the raincoat.

She sat down at a writing-desk, in the waiting-room, and wrote: "I am safe, and I thank you." Then she paused an instant, and with nervous haste wrote "Mary" underneath. She opened the suit-case and pinned the paper to the lapel of the evening coat. Just three dollars and sixty-seven cents she had left in her pocket-book after paying the expressage on the suit-case.

She felt doubtful whether she might not have done wrong about thus sending her dress back, but what else could she have done? If she had bought a box in which to put it, she would have had to carry it with her, and perhaps the dress might have been found during her absence from her room, and she suspected because of it. At any rate, it was too late now, and she felt sure the young man would understand. She hoped it would not inconvenience him especially to get rid of it. Surely he could give it to some charitable organization without much trouble.

At her first waking, in the early gray hours of the morning, she had looked her predicament calmly in the face. It was entirely likely that it would continue indefinitely; it might be, throughout her whole life. She could now see no way of help for herself. Time might, perhaps, give her a friend who would assist her, or a way might open back into her old life in some unthought-of manner, but for a time there must be hiding and a way found to earn her living.

She had gone carefully over her own accomplishments. Her musical attainments, which would naturally have been the first thought, were out of the question. Her skill as a musician was so great, and so well known by her enemy, that she would probably be traced by it at once. As she looked back at the hour spent at Mrs. Bowman's piano, she shuddered at the realization that it might have been her undoing, had it chanced that her enemy passed the house, with a suspicion that she was inside. She would never dare to seek a position as accompanist, and she knew how futile it would be for her to attempt to teach music in an unknown city, among strangers. She might starve to death before a single pupil appeared. Besides, that too would put her in a position where she would be more easily found. The same arguments were true if she were to attempt to take a position as teacher or governess, although she was thoroughly competent to do so. Rapidly rejecting all the natural resources which under ordinary circumstances she would have used to maintain herself, she determined to change her station entirely, at least for the present. She would have chosen to do something in a little, quiet hired room somewhere, sewing or decorating or something of the sort, but that too would be hopelessly out of her reach, without friends to aid her. A servant's place in some one's home was the only thing possible that presented itself to her mind. She could not cook, nor do general housework, but she thought she could fill the place of waitress.

With a brave face, but a shrinking heart, she stepped into a drug-store and looked up in the directory the addresses of several employment agencies.

6

IT was half past eleven when she stepped into the first agency on her list, and business was in full tide.

While she stood shrinking by the door the eyes of a dozen women fastened upon her, each with keen scrutiny. The sensitive color stole into her delicate cheeks. As the proprietress of the office began to question her, she felt her courage failing.

"You wish a position?" The woman had a nose like a hawk, and eyes that held no sympathy. "What do you want? General housework?"

"I should like a position as waitress." Her voice was low and sounded frightened to herself.

The hawk nose went up contemptuously.

"Better take general housework. There are too many waitresses already."

"I understand the work of a waitress, but I never have done general housework," she answered with the voice of a gentlewoman, which somehow angered the hawk, who had trained herself to get the advantage over people and keep it or else know the reason why.

"Very well, do as you please, of course, but you bite your own nose off. Let me see your references."

The girl was ready for this.

"I am sorry, but I cannot give you any. I have lived only in one home, where I had entire charge of the table and dining-room, and that home was broken up when the people went abroad three years ago. I could show you letters written by the mistress of that home if I had my trunk here, but it is in another city, and I do not know when I shall be able to send for it."

"No references!" screamed the hawk, then raising her voice, although it was utterly unnecessary: "Ladies, here is a girl who has no references. Do any of you want to venture?" The contemptuous laugh that followed had the effect of a warning to every woman in the room. "And this girl scorns general housework, and presumes to dictate for a place as a waitress," went on the hawk.

"I want a waitress badly," said a troubled woman in a subdued whisper, "but I really wouldn't dare take a girl without references. She might be a thief, you know, and then—really, she doesn't look as if she was used to houses like mine. I must have a neat, stylish-looking girl. No self-respecting waitress nowadays would go out in the street dressed like that."

All the eyes in the room seemed boring through the poor girl as she stood trembling, humiliated, her cheeks burning, while horrified tears demanded to be let up into her eyes. She held her dainty head proudly, and turned away with dignity.

"However, if you care to try," called out the hawk, "you can register at the desk and leave two dollars, and if in the meantime you can think of anybody who'll give us a reference, we'll look it up. But we never guarantee girls without references."

The tears were too near the surface now for her even to

acknowledge this information flung at her in an unpleasant voice. She went out of the office, and immediately,— surreptitiously,—two women hurried after her.

One was flabby, large, and overdressed, with a pasty complexion and eyes like a fish, in which was a lack of all moral sense. She hurried after the girl and took her by the shoulder just as she reached the top of the stairs that led down into the street.

The other was a small, timid woman, with anxiety and indecision written all over her, and a last year's street suit with the sleeves remodelled. When she saw who had stopped the girl, she lingered behind in the hall and pretended there was something wrong with the braid on her skirt. While she lingered she listened.

"Wait a minute, Miss," said the flashy woman. "You needn't feel bad about having references. Everybody isn't so particular. You come with me, and I'll put you in the way of earning more than you can ever get as a waitress. You weren't cut out for work, any way, with that face and voice. I've been watching you. You were meant for a lady. You need to be dressed up, and you'll be a real pretty girl—"

As she talked, she had come nearer, and now she leaned over and whispered so that the timid woman, who was beginning dimly to perceive what manner of creature this other woman was, could not hear.

But the girl stepped back with sudden energy and flashing eyes, shaking off the be-ringed hand that had grasped her shoulder.

"Don't you dare to speak to me!" she said in a loud, clear voice. "Don't you dare to touch me! You are a wicked woman! If you touch me again, I will go in there and tell all those women how you have insulted me!"

"Oh, well, if you're a saint, starve!" hissed the woman.

"I should rather starve ten thousand times than take help

from you," said the girl, and her clear, horrified eyes seemed to burn into the woman's evil face. She turned and slid away, like the wily old serpent that she was.

Down the stairs like lightning sped the girl, her head up in pride and horror, her eyes still flashing. And down the stairs after her sped the little, anxious woman, panting and breathless, determined to keep her in sight till she could decide whether it was safe to take a girl without a character—yet who had just shown a bit of her character unaware.

Two blocks from the employment office the girl paused, to realize that she was walking blindly, without any destination. She was trembling so with terror that she was not sure whether she had the courage to enter another office, and a long vista of undreamed-of fears arose in her imagination.

The little woman paused, too, eyeing the girl cautiously, then began in an eager voice:

"I've been following you."

The girl started nervously, a cold chill of fear coming over her. Was this a woman detective?

"I heard what that awful woman said to you, and I saw how you acted. You must be a good girl, or you wouldn't have talked to her that way. I suppose I'm doing a dangerous thing, but I can't help it. I believe you're all right, and I'm going to try you, if you'll take general housework. I need somebody right away, for I'm going to have a dinner party to-morrow night, and my girl left me this morning."

The kind tone in the midst of her troubles brought tears to the girl's eyes.

"Oh, thank you!" she said as she brushed the tears away. "I'm a stranger here, and I have never before been among strangers this way. I'd like to come and work for you, but I couldn't do general housework, I'm sure. I never did it, and I wouldn't know how."

"Can't you cook a little? I could teach you my ways."

"I don't know the least thing about cooking. I never cooked a thing in my life."

"What a pity! What was your mother thinking about? Every girl ought to be brought up to know a little about cooking, even if she does have some other employment."

"My mother has been dead a good many years." The tears brimmed over now, but the girl tried to smile. "I could help you with your dinner party," she went on. "That is, I know all about setting the tables and arranging the flowers and favors. I could paint the place-cards, too— I've done it many a time. And I could wait on the table. But I couldn't cook even an oyster."

"Oh, place-cards!" said the little woman, her eyes brightening. She caught at the word as though she had descried a new star in the firmament. "I wish I could have them. They cost so much to buy. I might have my washer-woman come and help with the cooking. She cooks pretty well, and I could help her beforehand, but she couldn't wait on table, to save her life. I wonder if you know much about menus. Could you help me fix out the courses and say what you think I ought to have, or don't you know about that? You see, I have this very particular company coming, and I want to have things nice. I don't know them very well. My husband has business relations with them and wants them invited, and of all times for Betty to leave this was the worst!" She had unconsciously fallen into a tone of equality with the strange girl.

"I should like to help you," said the girl, "but I must find somewhere to stay before night, and if I find a place I must take it. I just came to the city this morning, and have nowhere to stay overnight."

The troubled look flitted across the woman's face for a moment, but her desire got the better of her.

"I suppose my husband would think I was crazy to do it," she said aloud, "but I just can't help trusting you. Suppose you come and stay with me to-day and to-morrow, and help me out with this dinner party, and you can stay overnight at my house and sleep in the cook's room. If I like your work, I'll give you a recommendation as waitress. You can't get a good place anywhere without it, not from the offices, I'm sure. A recommendation ought to be worth a couple of days' work to you. I'd pay you something besides, but I really can't afford it, for the washerwoman charges a dollar and a half a day when she goes out to cook; but if you get your board and lodging and a reference, that ought to pay you."

"You are very kind," said the girl. "I shall be glad to do that."

"When will you come? Can you go with me now, or have you got to go after your things?"

"I haven't any things but these," she said simply, "and perhaps you will not think I am fine enough for your dinner party. I have a little money. I could buy a white apron. My trunk is a good many miles away, and I was in desperate straits and had to leave it."

"H'm! A stepmother, probably," thought the kindly little woman. "Poor child! She doesn't look as if she was used to roughing it. If I could only hold on to her and train her, she might be a treasure, but there's no telling what John will say. I won't tell him anything about her, if I can help it, till the dinner is over."

Aloud she said: "Oh, that won't be necessary. I've got a white apron I'll lend you—perhaps I'll give it to you if you do your work well. Then we can fix up some kind of a waitress's cap out of a lace-edged handkerchief, and you'll look fine. I'd rather do that and have you come right along home with me, for everything is at sixes and sevens. Betty went off without washing the breakfast dishes. You can wash dishes, any way."

"Why, I can try," laughed the girl, the ridiculousness of her present situation suddenly getting the better of other emotions.

And so they got into a car and were whirled away into a pretty suburb. The woman, whose name was Mrs. Hart, lived in a common little house filled with imitation oriental rugs and cheap furniture.

The two went to work at once, bringing order out of the confusion that reigned in the tiny kitchen. In the afternoon the would-be waitress sat down with a box of watercolors to paint dinner-cards, and as her skillful brush brought into being dainty landscapes, lovely flowers, and little brown birds, she pondered the strangeness of her lot.

The table the next night was laid with exquisite care, the scant supply of flowers having been used to best advantage, and everything showing the touch of a skilled hand. The long hours that Mrs. Hart had spent puckering her brow over the household department of fashion magazines helped her to recognize the fact that in her new maid she had what she was pleased to call "the real thing."

She sighed regretfully when the guest of honor, Mrs. Rhinehart, spoke of the deftness and pleasant appearance of her hostess's waitress.

"Yes," Mrs. Hart said, swelling with pride, "she is a treasure. I only wish I could keep her."

"She's going to get married, I suppose. They all do when they're good," sympathized the guest.

"No, but she simply won't do cooking, and I really haven't work enough for two servants in this little house."

The guest sat up and took notice.

"You don't mean to tell me that you are letting a girl like that slip through your fingers? I wish I had known about her. I have spent three days in intelligence offices. Is there any chance for me, do you think?"

Then did the little woman prove that she should have had an *e* in her name, for she burst into a most voluble account of the virtues of her new maid, until the other woman was ready to hire her on the spot. The result of it all was that "Mary" was summoned to an interview with

Mrs. Rhinehart in the dining-room, and engaged at four dollars a week, with every other Sunday afternoon and every other Thursday out, and her uniforms furnished.

The next morning Mr. Hart gave her a dollar-bill and told her that he appreciated the help she had given them, and wanted to pay her something for it.

She thanked him graciously and took the money with a kind of awe. Her first earnings! It seemed so strange to think that she had really earned some money, she who had always had all she wanted without lifting a finger.

She went to a store and bought a hair-brush and a few little things that she felt were necessities, with a fifty-cent straw telescope in which to put them. Thus, with her modest baggage, she entered the home of Mrs. Rhinehart, and ascended to a tiny room on the fourth floor, in which were a cot and a washstand, a cracked mirror, one chair, and one window. Mrs. Rhinehart had planned that the waitress should room with the cook, but the girl had insisted that she must have a room alone, no matter how small, and they had compromised on this unused, ill-furnished spot.

As she took off the felt hat, she wondered what its owner would think if he could see her now, and she brushed a fleck of dust gently from the felt, as if in apology for its humble surroundings. Then she smoothed her hair, put on the apron Mrs. Hart had given her, and descended to her new duties as maid in a fashionable home.

7

THREE days later Tryon Dunham entered the office of Judge Blackwell by appointment. After the business was completed the Judge said with a smile, "Well, our mystery is solved. The little girl is all safe. She telephoned me just after you had left the other day, and sent her maid after her hat. It seems that while she stood by the window, looking down into the street, she saw an automobile containing some of her friends. It stopped at the next building. Being desirous of speaking with a girl friend who was seated in the auto, she hurried out to the elevator, hoping to catch them. The elevator boy who took her down-stairs went off duty immediately, which accounts for our not finding any trace of her, and he was kept at home by illness the next morning. The young woman caught her friends, and they insisted that she should get in and ride to the station with one of them who was leaving the city at once. They loaned her a veil and a wrap, and promised to bring her right back for her papers and other possessions, but the train was late, and when they returned the building was closed. The two men who called for her were her brother and a friend of his, it seems. I must say they were not so attractive as she is. However, the mystery is solved, and I got well laughed at by my wife for my fears."

But the young man was puzzling how this all could be if the hat belonged to the girl he knew—to "Mary." When he left the Judge's office, he went to his club, determined to have a little quiet for thinking it over.

Matters at home had not been going pleasantly. There had been an ominous cloud over the breakfast table. The bill for the hat had arrived from Madame Dollard's, and Cornelia had laid it impressively by his plate. Even his mother had looked at him with a glance that spoke volumes as she remarked that it would be necessary for her to have a new rain-coat before another storm came.

There had been a distinct coolness between Tryon Dunham and his mother and sister ever since the morning when the loss of the hat and rain-coat was announced. Or did it date from the evening of that day when both mother and sister had noticed the beautiful ring which he wore? They had exclaimed over the flash of the diamond, and its peculiar pureness and brilliancy, and Cornelia had been quite disagreeable when he refused to take it off for her to examine. He had replied to his mother's question by saying that the ring belonged to a friend of his. He knew his mother was hurt by the answer, but what more could he do at present? True, he might have taken the ring off and prevented further comment, but it had come to him to mean loyalty to and belief in the girl whom he had so strangely been permitted to help. It was therefore in deep perplexity that he betook himself to his club and sat down in a far corner to meditate. He was annoyed when the office-boy appeared to tell him there were some packages awaiting him in the office.

"Bring them to me here, Henry."

The boy hustled away, and soon came back, bearing two hat-boxes—one of them in a crate—and the heavy leather suit-case.

With a start of surprise, Dunham sat up in his comfortable chair.

"Say, Henry, those things ought not to come in here." He glanced anxiously about, and was relieved to find that there was only one old gentleman in the room, and that he was asleep. "Suppose we go up to a private room with them. Take them out to the elevator, and I'll come in a moment."

"All right, sah."

"And say, Henry, suppose you remove that crate from the box. Then it won't be so heavy to carry."

"All right, sah. I'll be thah in jest a minute."

The young man hurried out to the elevator, and he and Henry made a quick ascent to a private room. He gave the boy a round fee, and was left in quiet to examine his property.

As he fumbled with the strings of the first box his heart beat wildly, and he felt the blood mounting to his face. Was he about to solve the mystery which had surrounded the girl in whom his interest had now grown so deep that he could scarcely get her out of his mind for a few minutes at a time?

But the box was empty, save for some crumpled white tissue-paper. He took up the cover in perplexity and saw his own name written by himself. Then he remembered. This was the box he had sent down to the club by the cabman, to get it out of his way. He felt disappointed, and turned quickly to the other box and cut the cord. This time he was rewarded by seeing the great black hat, beautiful and unhurt in spite of its journey to Chicago. The day was saved, and also the reputation of his mother's maid. But was there no word from the beautiful stranger? He searched hurriedly through the wrappings, pulled out the hat quite unceremoniously, and turned the box upside down, but nothing else could he find. Then he went at the suit-case. Yes, there was the raincoat. He took it out triumphantly, for now his mother could say nothing, and, moreover, was not his trust in the fair stranger justified? He had done well to believe in her. He began to take out the other garments, curious to see what had been there for her use.

A long, golden brown hair nestling on the collar of the bathrobe gleamed in a chance ray of sunlight. He looked at it reverently, and laid the garment down carefully, that it might not be disturbed. As he lifted the coat, he saw the little note pinned to the lapel, and seized it eagerly. Surely this would tell him something!

But no, there was only the message that she had arrived safely, and her thanks. Still, she had signed her name "Mary." She had told him he might call her that. Could it be that it was her real name, and that she had meant to trust him with so much of her true story?

He pondered the delicate writing of the note, thinking how like her it seemed, then he put the note in an inner pocket and thoughtfully lifted out the evening clothes. It was then that he touched the silken lined cloth of her dress, and he drew back almost as if he had ventured roughly upon something sacred. Startled, awed, he looked upon it, and then with gentle fingers lifted it and laid it upon his knee. Her dress! The one she had worn to the dinner with him! What did it all mean? Why was it here, and where was she?

He spread it out across his lap and looked at it almost as if it hid her presence. He touched with curious, wistful fingers the lace and delicate garniture about the waist, as if he would appeal to it to tell the story of her who had worn it.

What did its presence here mean? Did it bear some message? He searched carefully, but found nothing further. Had she reached a place of safety where she did not need the dress? No, for in that case, why should she have sent it to him? Had she been desperate perhaps, and—? But no, he would not think such things of her.

Gradually, as he looked, the gown told its own story, as she had thought it would: how she had been obliged to put on a disguise, and this was the only way to hide her own dress. Gradually he came to feel a great pleasure in the fact that she had trusted him with it. She had known he would understand, and perhaps had not had time to make further explanation. But if she had need of a disguise, she was still in danger! Oh, why had she not given him some clue? He dropped his head upon his hand in troubled perplexity.

A faint perfume of violets stole upon his senses from the dress lying across his knee. He touched it tenderly, and then half shame-facedly laid his cheek against it, breathing in the perfume. But he put it down quickly, looking quite foolish, and reminded himself that the girl was still a stranger, and that she might belong to another.

Then he thought again of the story the Judge had told him, and of his own first conviction that the two young women were identical. Could that be? Why could he not discover who the other girl was, and get some one to introduce him? He resolved to interview the Judge about it at their next meeting. In the meantime, he must wait and hope for further word from Mary. Surely she would write him again, and claim her ring perhaps, and, as she had been so thoughtful about returning the hat and coat at once, she would probably return the money he had loaned her. At least, he would hear from her in that way. There was nothing to do but be patient.

Yes, there was the immediate problem of how he should restore his sister's hat and his mother's coat to their places, unsuspected.

With a sigh, he carefully folded up the cloth gown, wrapped it in folds of tissue paper from the empty hat-box, and placed it in his suit-case. Then he transferred the hat to its original box, rang the bell, and ordered the boy to care for the box and suit-case until he called for them.

During the afternoon he took occasion to run into the

Judge's office about some unimportant detail of the business they were transacting, and as he was leaving he said:

"By the way, Judge, who was your young woman who gave you such a fright by her sudden disappearance? You never told me her name. Is she one of my acquaintances, I wonder?"

"Oh, her name is Mary Weston," said the Judge, smiling. "I don't believe you know her, for she was from California, and was visiting here only for a few days. She sailed for Europe the next day."

That closed the incident and, so far as the mystery was concerned, only added perplexity to it.

Dunham purposely remained down-town, merely having a clerk telephone home for him that he had gone out of the city and would not be home until late, so they need not wait up. He did this because he did not wish to have his mother or his sister ask him any more questions about the missing hat and coat. Then he took a twenty-mile trolley ride into the suburbs and back, to make good his word that he had gone out of town; and all the way he kept turning over and over the mystery of the beautiful young woman, until it began to seem to him that he had been crazy to let her drift out into the world alone and practically penniless. The dress had told its tale. He saw, of course, that if she were afraid of detection, she must have found it necessary to buy other clothing, and how could she have bought it with only nine dollars and seventy-five cents? He now felt convinced that he should have found some way to cash a check and thus supply her with what she needed. It was terrible. True, she had those other beautiful rings, which were probably valuable, but would she dare to sell them? Perhaps, though, she had found some one else as ready as he had been to help her. But, to his surprise, that thought was distasteful to him. During his long, cold ride in solitude he discovered that the thing he wanted most in life was to find that girl again and take care of her.

Of course he reasoned with himself most earnestly from one end of the trolley line to the other, and called himself all kinds of a fool, but it did not the slightest particle of good. Underneath all the reasoning, he knew he was glad that he had found her once, and he determined to find her again, and to unravel the mystery. Then he sat looking long and earnestly into the depths of the beautiful white stone she had given to him, as if he might there read the way to find her.

A little after midnight he arrived at the club-house, secured his suit-case and the hat-box, and took a cab to his home. He left the vehicle at the corner, lest the sound of it waken his mother or sister.

He let himself silently into the house with his latch-key, and tiptoed up to his room. The light was burning low. He put the hat-box in the farthest corner of his closet, then he took out the rain-coat, and, slipping off his shoes, went softly down to the hall closet.

In utter darkness he felt around and finally hung the coat on a hook under another long cloak, then gently released the hanging loop and let the garment slip softly down in an inconspicuous heap on the floor. He stole upstairs as guiltily as if he had been a naughty boy stealing sugar. When he reached his room, he turned up his light, and, pulling out the hat-box, surveyed it thoughtfully. This was a problem which he had not yet been able to solve. How should he dispose of the hat so that it would be discovered in such a way as to cast no further suspicion upon the maid? How would it do to place the hat in the hall-closet, back among the coats? No, it might excite suspicion to find them together. Could he put it in his own closet and profess to have found it there? No, for that might lead to unpleasant questioning, and perhaps involve the servants again. If he could only put it back where he had found it! But Cornelia, of course, would know it had not been there in her room all this week. It would be better to wait until the coast was clear and hide it in Cornelia's closet, where it might have been put by mistake and forgotten. It was going to be hard to explain, but that was the best plan he could evolve.

He took the hat out and held it on his hand, looking at it from different angles and trying to remember just how the girl had looked out at him from under its drooping plumes. Then with a sigh he laid it carefully in its box again and went to bed.

The morning brought clearer thought, and when the summons to breakfast pealed through the hall he took the box boldly in his hand and descended to the dining-room, where he presented the hat to his astonished sister.

"I am afraid I am the criminal, Cornelia," he said in his pleasantest manner. "I'm sorry I can't explain just how this thing got on my closet-shelf. I must have put it there myself through some unaccountable mix-up. It's too bad I couldn't have found it before and so saved you a lot of worry. But you are one hat the richer for it, for I paid the bill yesterday. Please accept it with my compliments."

Cornelia exclaimed with delight over the recovered hat.

"But how in the world could it have got into your closet, Tryon? It was impossible. I left it my room, I know I did, for I spoke to Norah about it before I left. How do you account for it?"

"Oh, I don't attempt to account for it," he said, with a gay wave of his hand. "I've been so taken up with other things this past week, I may have done almost anything. By the way, Mother, I'm sure you'll be glad to hear that Judge Blackwell has made me a most generous offer of business relations, and that I have decided to accept it."

Amid the exclamations of delight over this bit of news, the hat was forgotten for a time, and when the mother and sister finally reverted to it and began to discuss how it could have gotten on the closet shelf, he broke in upon their questions with a suggestion.

"I should advise, Mother, that you make a thorough search for your rain-coat. I am sure now that you must have overlooked it. Such things often happen. We were so excited the morning Cornelia missed the hat that I suppose no one looked thoroughly."

"But that is impossible, Tryon," said his mother, with dignity. "I had that closet searched most carefully."

"Nevertheless, Mother, please me by looking again. That closet is dark, and I would suggest a light."

"Of course, if you wish it," said his mother stiffly. "You might look, yourself."

"I'm afraid I shall not have time this morning," professed the coward. "But suppose you look in your own closets, too, Mother. I'm sure you'll find it somewhere. It couldn't get out of the house of itself, and Norah is no thief. The idea is preposterous. Please have it attended to carefully to-day. Good-by. I shall have to hurry downtown, and I can't tell just what time I shall get back this evening. 'Phone me if you find the coat anywhere. If you don't find it, I'll buy you another this afternoon."

"I shall *not* find the rain-coat," said his mother sternly, "but of course I will look to satisfy you. I *know* it is not in this house."

He beat a hasty retreat, for he did not care to be present at the finding of the rain-coat.

"There is something strange about this," said Mrs. Dunham, as with ruffled dignity she emerged from the hall closet, holding her lost rain-coat at arm's length. "You don't suppose your brother could be playing some kind of a joke on us, do you, Cornie? I never did understand jokes."

"Of course not," said practical Cornelia, with a sniff. "It's my opinion that Norah knows all about the matter, and Tryon has been helping her out with a few suggestions."

"Now, Cornelia, what do you mean by that? You surely don't suppose your brother would try to deceive us—his mother and sister?"

"I didn't say that, Mother," answered Cornelia, with her head in the air. "You've got your rain-coat back, but you'd better watch the rest of your wardrobe. I don't intend to let Norah have free range in my room any more."

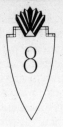

8

MEANTIME, the girl in Chicago was walking in a new and hard way. She brought to her task a disciplined mind, a fine artistic taste, a delicate but healthy body, and a pair of willing, if unskilled, hands. To her surprise, she discovered that the work for which she had so often lightly given orders was beyond her strength. Try as she would, she could not accomplish the task of washing and ironing table napkins and delicate embroidered linen pieces in the way she knew they should be done. Will power can accomplish a good deal, but it cannot always make up for ignorance, and the girl who had mastered difficult subjects in college, and astonished music masters in the old world with her talent, found that she could not wash a window even to her own satisfaction, much less to that of her new mistress. That these tasks were expected of her was a surprise. Yet with her ready adaptability and her strong good sense, she saw that if she was to be a success in this new field she had chosen, she must be ready for any emergency. Nevertheless, as the weary days succeeded each other into weeks, she found that while her skill in table-setting and waiting was much prized, it was more than offset by her discrepancies in other lines, and so it came about that with mutual consent she and Mrs. Rhinehart parted company.

This time, with her reference, she did not find it so hard to get another place, and, after trying several, she learned to demand certain things, which put her finally into a home where her ability was appreciated, and where she was not required to do things in which she was unskilled.

She was growing more secure in her new life now, and less afraid to venture into the streets lest some one should be on the watch for her. But night after night, as she climbed to her cheerless room and crept to her scantily-covered, uncomfortable couch, she shrank from all that life could now hold out to her. Imprisoned she was, to a narrow round of toil, with no escape, and no one to know or care. And who knew but that any day an enemy might trace her?

Then the son of the house came home from college in disgrace, and began to make advances to her, until her case seemed almost desperate. She dreaded inexpressibly to make another change, for in some ways her work was not so hard as it had been in other places, and her wages were better; but from day to day she felt she could scarcely bear the hourly annoyances. The other servants, too, were not only utterly uncompanionable, but deeply jealous of her, resenting her gentle breeding, her careful speech, her dainty personal ways, her room to herself, her loyalty to her mistress.

Sometimes in the cold and darkness of the night-vigils she would remember the man who had helped her, and who had promised to be her friend, and had begged her to let him know if she ever needed help. Her hungry heart cried out for sympathy and counsel. In her dreams she saw him coming to her across interminable plains, hastening with his kindly sympathy, but she always awoke before he reached her.

9

IT was about this time that the firm of Blackwell, Hanover
& Dunham had a difficult case to work out which involved
the gathering of evidence from Chicago and thereabouts,
and it was with pleasure that Judge Blackwell accepted the
eager proposal from the junior member of the firm that he
should go out and attend to it.

As Tryon Dunham entered the sleeper, and placed his
suit-case beside him on the seat, he was reminded of the
night when he had taken this train with the girl who had
come to occupy a great part of his thoughts in these days.
He had begun to feel that if he could ever hope to shake off
his anxiety and get back to his normal state of mind, he
must find her and unravel the mystery about her. If she
were safe and had friends, so that he was not needed, perhaps he would be able to put her out of his thoughts, but if
she were not safe—— He did not quite finish the sentence
even in his thoughts, but his heart beat quicker always, and
he knew that if she needed him he was ready to help her,
even at the sacrifice of his life.

All during the journey he planned a campaign for finding her, until he came to know in his heart that this was the

real mission for which he had come to Chicago, although he intended to perform the other business thoroughly and conscientiously.

Upon his arrival in Chicago, he inserted a number of advertisements in the daily papers, having laid various plans by which she might safely communicate with him without running the risk of detection by her enemy.

> If M.R. is in Chicago, will she kindly communicate with T. Dunham, General Delivery? Important.

> Mrs. Bowman's friend has something of importance to say to the lady who dined with her October 8th. Kindly send address to T.D., Box 7 *Inter-Ocean* office.

> "Mary," let me know where and when I can speak with you about a matter of importance. Tryon D., *Record-Herald* L.

These and others appeared in the different papers, but when he began to get communications from all sorts of poor creatures, every one demanding money, and when he found himself running wild-goose chases after different Marys and M.R.s, he abandoned all hope of personal columns in the newspapers. Then he began a systematic search for music teachers and musicians, for it seemed to him that this would be her natural way of earning her living, if she were so hard pressed that this was necessary.

In the course of his experiments he came upon many objects of pity, and his heart was stirred with the sorrow and the misery of the human race as it had never been stirred in all his happy, well-groomed life. Many a poor soul was helped and strengthened and put into the way of doing better because of this brief contact with him. But always as he saw new miseries he was troubled over what might have become of her—"Mary." It came to pass that whenever he looked upon the face of a young woman, no matter how pinched and worn with poverty, he dreaded lest *she* might have come to this pass, and be in actual need. As these thoughts went on day by day, he came to feel that she was his by a God-given right, his to find, his to care for. If she was in peril, he must save her. If she had done wrong—but this he could never believe. Her face was too pure and lovely for that. So the burden of her weighed upon his heart all the days while he went about the difficult business of gathering evidence link by link in the important law case that had brought him to Chicago.

Dunham had set apart working hours, and he seemed to labor with double vigor then because of the other task he had set for himself. When at last he finished the legal business he had come for, and might go home, he lingered yet a day, and then another, devoting himself with almost feverish activity to the search for his unknown friend.

It was the evening of the third day after his law work was finished that with a sad heart he went toward the hotel where he had been stopping. He was obliged at last to face the fact that his search had been in vain.

He had almost reached the hotel when he met a business acquaintance, who welcomed him warmly, for far and wide among legal men the firm of which Judge Blackwell was the senior member commanded respect.

"Well, well!" said the older man. "Is this you, Dunham? I thought you were booked for home two days ago. Suppose you come home to dinner with me. I've a matter I'd like to talk over with you before you leave. I shall count this a most fortunate meeting if you will."

Just because he caught at any straw to keep him longer in Chicago, Dunham accepted the invitation. Just as the cab door was flung open in front of the handsome house where he was to be a guest, two men passed slowly by, like shadows out of place, and there floated to his ears one sentence voiced in broadest Irish: "She goes by th' name of

Mary, ye says? All roight, sorr. I'll keep a sharp lookout."

Tryon Dunham turned and caught a glimpse of silver changing hands. One man was slight and fashionably dressed, and the light that was cast from the neighboring window showed his face to be dark and handsome. The other was short and stout, and clad in a faded Prince Albert coat that bagged at shoulders and elbows. He wore rubbers over his shoes, and his footsteps sounded like those of a heavy dog. The two passed around the corner, and Dunham and his host entered the house.

They were presently seated at a well appointed table, where an elaborate dinner was served. The talk was of pleasant things that go to make up the world of refinement; but the mind of the guest was troubled, and constantly kept hearing that sentence, "She goes by the name of Mary."

Then, suddenly, he looked up and met her eyes!

She was standing just back of her mistress's chair, with quiet, watchful attitude, but her eyes had been unconsciously upon the guest, until he looked up and caught her glance.

She turned away, but the color rose in her cheeks, and she knew that he was watching her.

Her look had startled him. He had never thought of looking for her in a menial position, and at first he had noticed only the likeness to her for whom he was searching. But he watched her furtively, until he became more and more startled with the resemblance.

She did not look at him again, but he noticed that her cheeks were scarlet, and that the long lashes drooped as if she were trying to hide her eyes. She went now and again from the room on her silent, deft errands, bringing and taking dishes, filling the glasses with ice water, seeming to know at a glance just what was needed. Whenever she went from the room he tried to persuade himself that it was not she, and then became feverishly impatient for her return that he might anew convince himself that it *was*. He felt a helpless rage at the son of the house for the familiar way in which he said: "Mary, fill my glass," and could not keep from frowning. Then he was startled at the similarity of names. Mary! The men on the street had used the name, too! Could it be that her enemy had tracked her? Perhaps he, Dunham, had appeared just in time to help her! His busy brain scarcely heard the questions with which his host was plying him, and his replies were distraught and monosyllabic. At last he broke in upon the conversation:

"Excuse me, but I wonder if I may interrupt you for a moment. I have thought of something that I ought to attend to at once. I wonder if the waitress would be kind enough to send a 'phone message for me. I am afraid it will be too late if I wait."

"Why, certainly," said the host, all anxiety. "Would you like to go to the 'phone yourself, or can I attend to it for you? Just feel perfectly at home."

Already the young man was hastily writing a line or two on a card he had taken from his pocket, and he handed it to the waitress, who at his question had moved silently behind his chair to do his bidding.

"Just call up that number, please, and give the message below. They will understand, and then you will write down their answer?"

He handed her the pencil and turned again to his dessert, saying with a relieved air:

"Thank you. I am sorry for the interruption. Now will you finish that story?" Apparently his entire attention was devoted to his host and his ice, but in reality he was listening to the click of the telephone and the low, gentle voice in an adjoining room. It came after only a moment's pause, and he wondered at the calmness with which the usual formula of the telephone was carried on. He could not hear what she said, but his ears were alert to the pause, just long enough for a few words to be written, and then to her footsteps coming quietly back.

His heart was beating wildly. It seemed to him that his host must see the strained look in his face, but he tried to fasten his interest upon the conversation and keep calm.

He had applied the test. There was no number upon the card, and he knew that if the girl were not the one of whom he was in search, she would return for an explanation.

If you are Mary Remington tell me where and when I can talk with you. Immediately important to us both!

This was what he had written on the card. His fingers trembled as he took it from the silver tray which she presented to him demurely. He picked it up and eagerly read the delicate writing—hers—the same that had expressed her thanks and told of her safe arrival in Chicago. He could scarcely refrain from leaping from his chair and shouting aloud in his gladness.

The message she had written was simple. No stranger reading it would have thought twice about it. If the guest had read it aloud, it would have aroused no suspicion.

Y.W.C.A. Building, small parlor, three to-morrow.

He knew the massive building, for he had passed it many times, but never had he supposed it could have any interest for him. Now suddenly his heart warmed to the great organization of Christian women who had established these havens for homeless ones in the heart of the great cities.

He looked up at the girl as she was passing the coffee on the other side of the table, but not a flicker of an eyelash showed she recognized him. She went through her duties and withdrew from the room, but though they lingered long over the coffee, she did not return. When they went into the other room, his interest in the family grew less and less. The daughter of the house sat down at the piano, after leading him up to ask her to sing, and chirped through several sentimental songs, tinkling out a shallow accompaniment with her plump, manicured fingers. His soul revolted at the thought that she should be here entertaining the company, while that other one whose music would have thrilled them all stayed humbly in the kitchen, doing some menial task.

He took his leave early in the evening and hurried back to his hotel. As he crossed the street to hail a cab, he thought he saw a short, baggy figure shambling along in the shadow on the other side, looking up at the house.

He had professed to have business to attend to, but when he reached his room he could do nothing but sit down and think. That he had found her for whom he had so long sought filled him with a deeper joy than any he had ever known before. That he had found her in such a position deepened the mystery and filled him with a nameless dread. Then out of the shadow of his thoughts shambled the baggy man in the rubbers, and he could not rest, but took his hat and walked out again into the great rumbling whirl of the city night, walking on and on, until he again reached the house where he had dined.

He passed in front of the building, and found lights still burning everywhere. Down the side street, he saw the windows were brightly lighted in the servants' quarters, and loud laughter was sounding. Was she in there enduring such company? No, for there high in the fourth story gleamed a little light, and a shadow moved about across the curtain. Something told him that it was her room. He paced back and forth until the light went out, and then reverently, with lifted hat, turned and found his way back to the main avenue and a car line. As he passed the area gate a bright light shot out from the back door, there was a peal of laughter, an Irish goodnight, and a short man in baggy coat and rubbers shambled out and scuttled noiselessly down to the back street.

10

DUNHAM slept very little that night. His soul was hovering between joy and anxiety. Almost he was inclined to find some way to send her word about the man he had seen lingering about the place, and yet perhaps it was foolish. He had doubtless been to call on the cook, and there might be no connection whatever between what Dunham had heard and seen and the lonely girl.

Next day, with careful hands, the girl made herself neat and trim with the few materials she had at hand. Her own fine garments that had lain carefully wrapped and hidden ever since she had gone into service were brought forth, and the coarse ones with which she had provided herself against suspicion were laid aside. If any one came into her room while she was gone, he would find no fine French embroidery to tell tales. Also, she wished to feel as much like herself as possible, and she never could quite feel that in her cheap outfit. True, she had no finer outer garments than a cheap black flannel skirt and coat which she had bought with the first money she could spare, but they were warm, and answered for what she had needed. She had not bought a hat, and had nothing now to wear upon her head but the black felt that belonged to the man she was going to meet. She looked at herself pityingly in the tiny mirror, and wondered if the young man would understand and forgive? It was all she had, any way, and there would be no time to go to the store and buy another before the appointed hour, for the family had brought unexpected company to a late lunch and kept her far beyond her hour for going out.

She looked down dubiously at her shabby shoes, their delicate kid now cracked and worn. Her hands were covered by a pair of cheap black silk gloves. It was the first time that she had noticed these things so keenly, but now it seemed to her most embarrassing to go thus to meet the man who had helped her.

She gathered her little hoard of money to take with her, and cast one look back over the cheerless room, with a great longing to bid it farewell forever, and go back to the world where she belonged; yet she realized that it was a quiet refuge for her from the world that she must hereafter face. Then she closed her door, went down the stairs and out into the street, like any other servant on her afternoon out, walking away to meet whatever crisis might arise. She had not dared to speculate much about the subject of the coming interview. It was likely he wanted to inquire about her comfort, and perhaps offer material aid. She would not accept it, of course, but it would be a comfort to know that some one cared. She longed inexpressibly for this interview, just because he had been kind, and because he belonged to that world from which she had come. He would keep her secret. He had true eyes. She did not notice soft, padded feet that came wobbling down the street after her, and she only drew a little further out toward the curbing when a bleary-eyed, red face peered into hers as she stood waiting for the car. She did not notice the shabby man who boarded the car after she was seated.

Tryon Dunham stood in the great stone doorway, watching keenly the passing throng. He saw the girl at once as she got out of the car, but he did not notice the man in the baggy coat, who lumbered after her and watched with wondering scrutiny as Dunham came forward, lifted his hat, and took her hand respectfully. Here was an element he did not understand. He stood staring, puzzled, as they disappeared into the great building; then planted himself in a convenient place to watch until his charge should come out again. This was perhaps a gentleman who had come to engage her to work for him. She might be thinking of changing her place. He must be on the alert.

Dunham placed two chairs in the far corner of the inner parlor, where they were practically alone, save for an occasional passer through the hall. He put the girl into the most comfortable one, and then went to draw down the shade, to shut a sharp ray of afternoon sunlight from her eyes. She sat there and looked down upon her shabby shoes, her cheap gloves, her coarse garments, and honored him for the honor he was giving her in this attire. She had learned by sharp experience that such respect to one in her station was not common. As he came back, he stood a moment looking down upon her. She saw his eye rest with recognition upon the hat she wore, and her pale cheeks turned pink.

"I don't know what you will think of my keeping this," she said shyly, putting her hand to the hat, "but it seemed really necessary at the time, and I haven't dared spend the money for a new one yet. I thought perhaps you would forgive me, and let me pay you for it some time later."

"Don't speak of it," he broke in, in a low voice. "I am so glad you could use it at all. It would have been a comfort to me if I had known where it was. I had not even missed it, because at this time of year I have very little use for it. It is my traveling hat."

He looked at her again as though the sight of her was good to him, and his gaze made her quite forget the words she had planned to say.

"I am so glad I have found you!" he went on. "You have not been out of my thoughts since I left you that night on the train. I have blamed myself over and over again for having gone then. I should have found some way to stand by you. I have not had one easy moment since I saw you last."

His tone was so intense that she could not interrupt him; she could only sit and listen in wonder, half trembling, to the low-spoken torrent of feeling that he expressed. She tried to protest, but the look in his face stopped her. He went on with an earnestness that would not be turned aside from its purpose.

"I came to Chicago that I might search for you. I could not stand the suspense any longer. I have been looking for you in every way I could think of, without openly searching, for that I dared not do lest I might jeopardize your safety. I was almost in despair when I went to dine with Mr. Phillips last evening. I felt I could not go home without knowing at least that you were safe, and now that I have found you, I cannot leave you until I know at least that you have no further need for help."

She summoned her courage now, and spoke in a voice full of feeling:

"Oh, you must not feel that way. You helped me just when I did not know what to do, and put me in the way of helping myself. I shall never cease to thank you for your kindness to an utter stranger. And now I am doing very well." She tried to smile, but the tears came unbidden instead.

"You poor child!" His tone was full of something deeper than compassion, and his eyes spoke volumes. "Do you suppose I think you are doing well when I see you wearing the garb of a menial and working for people to whom you are far superior—people who by all the rights of education and refinement ought to be in the kitchen serving you?"

"It was the safest thing I could do, and really the only thing I could get to do at once," she tried to explain. "I'm doing it better every day."

"I have no doubt. You can be an artist at serving as well as anything else, if you try. But now that is all over. I am going to take care of you. There is no use in protesting. If I may not do it in one way, I will in another. There is one question I must ask first, and I hope you will trust me enough to answer it. Is there any other—any other man who has the right to care for you, and is unable or unwilling to do it?"

She looked up at him, her large eyes still shining with tears, and shuddered slightly.

"Oh, no!" she said. "Oh, no, I thank God there is not! My dear uncle has been dead for four years, and there has never been any one else who cared since Father died."

He looked at her, a great light beginning to come into his face; but she did not understand and turned her head to hide the tears.

"Then I am going to tell you something," he said, his tone growing lower, yet clear enough for her to hear every word distinctly.

A tall, oldish girl with a discontented upper lip stalked through the hall, glanced in at the door, and sniffed significantly, but they did not see her. A short, baggy-coated man outside hovered anxiously around the building and passed the very window of that room, but the shade opposite them was down, and they did not know. The low, pleasant voice went on:

"I have come to care a great deal for you since I first saw you, and I want you to give me the right to care for you always and protect you against the whole world."

She looked up, wonderingly.

"What do you mean?"

"I mean that I love you, and I want to make you my wife. Then I can defy the whole world if need be, and put you where you ought to be."

"Oh!" she breathed softly.

"Wait, please," he pleaded, laying his hand gently on her little, trembling one. "Don't say anything until I have finished. I know of course that this will be startling to you. You have been brought up to feel that such things must be more carefully and deliberately done. I do not want you to feel that this is the only way I can help you, either. If you are not willing to be my wife, I will find some other plan. But this is the best way, if it isn't too hard on you, for I love you as I never dreamed that I could love a woman. The only question is, whether you can put up with me until I can teach you to love me a little."

She lifted eloquent eyes to his face.

"Oh, it is not that," she stammered, a rosy light flooding cheek and brow. "It is not that at all. But you know nothing about me. If you knew, you would very likely think as others do, and——"

"Then do not tell me anything about yourself, if it will trouble you. I do not care what others think. If you have poisoned a husband, I should know that he needed poisoning, and any way I should love you and stand by you."

"I have not done anything wrong," she said gravely.

"Then if you have done nothing wrong, we will prove it to the world, or, if we cannot prove it, we will fly to some desert island and live there in peace and love. That is the way I feel about you. I know that you are good and true and lovely! Any one might as well try to prove to me that you were crazy as that you had done wrong in any way."

Her face grew strangely white.

"Well, suppose I was crazy?"

"Then I would take you and cherish you and try to cure

you, and if that could not be done, I should help you to
bear it."

"Oh, you are wonderful!" she breathed, the light of a
great love growing in her eyes.

The bare, prosaic walls stood stolidly about them, indif-
ferent to romance or tragedy that was being wrought out
within its walls. The whirl and hum of the city without,
the grime and soil of the city within, were alike forgotten
by these two as their hearts throbbed in the harmony of a
great passion.

"Do you think you could learn to love me?" said the
man's voice, with the sweetness of the love song of the
ages in its tone.

"I love you now," said the girl's low voice. "I think I
have loved you from the beginning, though I never dared
to think of it in that way. But it would not be right for me
to become your wife when you know practically nothing
about me."

"Have you forgotten that you know nothing of me?"

"Oh, I do know something about you," she said shyly.
"Remember that I have dined with your friends. I could
not help seeing that they were good people, especially that
delightful old man, the Judge. He looked startlingly like
my dear father. I saw how they all honored and loved you.
And then what you have done for me, and the way that
you treated an utterly defenceless stranger, were equal to
years of mere acquaintance. I feel that I know a great deal
about you."

He smiled. "Thank you," he said, "but I have not forgotten that something more is due you than that slight
knowledge of me, and before I came out here I went to the
pastor of the church of which my mother is a member, and
which I have always attended and asked him to write me a
letter. He is so widely known that I felt it would be an
introduction for me."

He laid an open letter in her lap, and, glancing down, she saw that it was signed by the name of one of the best known pulpit orators in the land, and that it spoke in highest terms of the young man whom it named as "my well-loved friend."

"It is also your right to know that I have always tried to live a pure and honorable life. I have never told any woman but you that I loved her—except an elderly cousin with whom I thought I was in love when I was nineteen. She cured me of it by laughing at me, and I have been heart-whole ever since."

She raised her eyes from reading the letter.

"You have all these, and I have nothing." She spread out her hands helplessly. "It must seem strange to you that I am in this situation. It does to me. It is awful."

She put her hands over her eyes and shuddered.

"It is to save you from it all that I have come." He leaned over and spoke tenderly, "Darling!"

"Oh, wait!" She caught her breath as if it hurt her, and put out her hand to stop him. "Wait! You must not say any more until I have told you all about it. Perhaps when I have told you, you will think about me as others do, and I shall have to run from you."

"Can you not trust me?" he reproached her.

"Oh, yes, I can trust you, but you may no longer trust me, and that I cannot bear."

"I promise you solemnly that I will believe every word you say."

"Ah, but you will think I do not know, and that it is your duty to give me into the hands of my enemies."

"That I most solemnly vow I will never do," he said earnestly. "You need not fear to tell me anything. But listen, tell me this one thing: in the eyes of God, is there any reason, physical, mental, or spiritual, why you should not become my wife?"

She looked at him clearly in the eyes.

"None at all."

"Then I am satisfied to take you without hearing your story until afterwards."

"But I am not satisfied. If I am to see distrust come into your eyes, it must be now, not afterwards."

"Then tell it quickly."

He put out his hand and took hers firmly into his own, as if to help her in her story.

"MY father died when I was only a young girl. We had not much money, and my mother's older brother took us to his home to live. My mother was his youngest sister, and he loved her more than any one else living. There was another sister, a half-sister, much older than my mother, and she had one son. He was a sulky, handsome boy, with a selfish, cruel nature. He seemed to be happy only when he was tormenting some one. He used to come to Uncle's to visit when I was there, and he delighted in annoying me. He stretched barbed wire where he knew I was going to pass in the dark, to throw me down and tear my clothes. He threw a quantity of burrs in my hair, and once he led me into a hornet's nest. After we went to live at my uncle's, Richard was not there so much. He had displeased my uncle, and he sent him away to school; but at vacation times he came again, and kept the house in discomfort. He seemed always to have a special spite against me. Once he broke a rare Dresden vase that Uncle prized, and told him I had done it.

"Mother did not live long after Father died, and after she was gone, I had no one to stand between me and Richard.

Sometimes I had to tell my uncle, but oftener I tried to bear it, because I knew Richard was already a great distress to him.

"At last Richard was expelled from college, and Uncle was so angry with him that he told him he would do nothing more for him. He must go to work. Richard's father and mother had not much money, and there were other children to support. Richard threatened me with all sorts of awful things if I did not coax Uncle to take him back into his good graces again. I told him I would not say a word to Uncle. He was very angry and swore at me. When I tried to leave the room he locked the door and would not let me go until I screamed for help. Then he almost choked me, but when he heard Uncle coming he jumped out of the window. The next day he forged a check in my uncle's name, and tried to throw suspicion on me, but he was discovered, and my uncle disinherited him. Uncle had intended to educate Richard and start him well in life, but now he would have nothing further to do with him. It seemed to work upon my uncle's health, all the disgrace to the family name, although no one ever thought of my uncle in connection with blame. As he paid Richard's debts, it was not known what the boy had done, except by the banker, who was a personal friend.

"We went abroad then, and everywhere Uncle amused himself by putting me under the best music masters, and giving me all possible advantages in languages, literature, and art. Three years ago he died at Carlsbad, and after his death I went back to my music studies, following his wishes in the matter, and staying with a dear old lady in Vienna, who had been kind to us when we were there before.

"As soon as my uncle's death was known at home, Richard wrote the most pathetic letter to me, professing deep contrition, and saying he could never forgive himself for having quarrelled with his dear uncle. He had a sad tale of how the business that he had started had failed and left him with debts. If he had only a few hundred dollars, he could go on with it and pay off everything. He said I had inherited all that would have been his if he had done right, and he recognized the justice of it, but begged that I would lend him a small sum until he could get on his feet, when he would repay me.

"I had little faith in his reformation, but felt as if I could not refuse him when I was enjoying what might have been his, so I sent him all the money I had at hand. As I was not yet of age, I could not control all the property, but my allowance was liberal. Richard continued to send me voluminous letters, telling of his changed life, and finally asked me to marry him. I declined emphatically, but he continued to write for money, always ending with a statement of his undying affection. In disgust, I at last offered to send him a certain sum of money regularly if he would stop writing to me on this subject, and finally succeeded in reducing our correspondence to a check account. This has been going on for three years, except that he has been constantly asking for larger sums, and whenever I would say that I could not spare more just then he would begin telling me how much he cared for me, and how hard it was for him to be separated from me. I began to feel desperate about him, and made up my mind that when I received the inheritance I should ask the lawyers to make some arrangement with him by which I should no longer be annoyed.

"It was necessary for me to return to America when I came of age, in order to sign certain papers and take full charge of the property. Richard knew this. He seems to have had some way of finding out everything my uncle did.

"He wrote telling me of a dear friend of his mother, who was soon to pass through Vienna, and who by some misfortune had been deprived of a position as companion and chaperon to a young girl who was travelling. He said it had occurred to him that perhaps he could serve us both by suggesting to me that she be my travelling companion on the voyage. He knew I would not want to travel alone, and he sent her address and all sorts of credentials, with a message from his mother that she would feel perfectly safe about me if I went in this woman's guardianship.

"I really did need a travelling companion, of course, having failed to get my dear old lady to undertake the voyage, so I thought it could do no harm. I went to see her, and found her pretty and frail and sad. She made a piteous appeal to me, and though I was not greatly taken with her, I decided she would do as well as any one for a companion.

"She did not bother me during the voyage, but fluttered about and was quite popular on board, especially with a tall, disagreeable man with a cruel jaw and small eyes, who always made me feel as if he would gloat over any one in his power. I found out that he was a physician, a specialist in mental diseases, so Mrs. Chambray told me, and she talked a great deal about his skill and insight into such maladies.

"At New York my cousin Richard met us and literally took possession of us. Without my knowledge, the cruel-looking doctor was included in the party. I did not discover it until we were on the train, bound, as I supposed, for my old home just beyond Buffalo. It was some time since I had been in New York, and I naturally did not notice much which way we were going. The fact was, every plan was anticipated, and I was told that all arrangements had been made. Mrs. Chambray began to treat me like a little child and say: 'You see we are going to take good care of you, dear, so don't worry about a thing.'

"I had taken the drawing-room compartment, not so much because I had a headache, as I told them, as because I wanted to get away from their society. My cousin's marked devotion became painful to me. Then, too, the attentions and constant watchfulness of the disagreeable doctor became most distasteful.

"We had been sitting on the observation platform, and it was late in the afternoon, when I said I was going to lie down, and the two men got up to go into the smoker. In spite of my protests, Mrs. Chambray insisted upon following me in, to see that I was perfectly comfortable. She fussed around me, covering me up and offering smelling salts and eau de cologne for my head. I let her fuss, thinking that was the quickest way to get rid of her. I closed my eyes, and she said she would go out to the observation platform. I lay still for awhile, thinking about her and how much I wanted to get rid of her. She acted as if she had been engaged to stay with me forever, and it suddenly became very plain to me that I ought to have a talk with her and tell her that I should need her services no longer after this journey was over. It might make a difference to her if she knew it at once, and perhaps now would be as good a time to talk as any, for she was probably alone out on the platform. I got up and made a few little changes in my dress, for it would soon be time to go into the dining-car. Then I went out to the observation platform, but she was not there. The chairs were all empty, so I chose the one next to the railing, away from the car door, and sat down to wait for her, thinking she would soon be back.

"We were going very fast, through a pretty bit of country. It was dusky and restful out there, so I leaned back and closed my eyes. Presently I heard voices approaching, above the rumble of the train, and, peeping around the doorway, I saw Mrs. Chambray, Richard, and the doctor coming from the other car. I kept quiet, hoping they would not come out, and they did not. They settled down near the door, and ordered the porter to put up a table for them to play cards.

"The train began to slow down, and finally came to a

halt for a longer time on a sidetrack, waiting for another train to pass. I heard Richard ask where I was. Mrs. Chambray said laughingly that I was safely asleep. Then, before I realized it, they began to talk about me. It happened there were no other passengers in the car. Richard asked Mrs. Chambray if she thought I had any suspicion that I was not on the right train, and she said, 'Not the slightest,' and then by degrees there floated to me through the open door the most diabolical plot I had ever heard of. I gathered from it that we were on the way to Philadelphia, would reach there in a little while, and would then proceed to a place near Washington, where the doctor had a private insane asylum, and where I was to be shut up. They were going to administer some drug that would make me unconscious when I was taken off the train. If they could not get me to take it for the headache I had talked about, Mrs. Chambray was to manage to get it into my food or give it to me when asleep. Mrs. Chambray, it seems, had not known the entire plot before leaving Europe, and this was their first chance of telling her. They thought I was safely in my compartment, asleep, and she had gone into the other car to give the signal as soon as she thought she had me where I would not get up again for a while.

"They had arranged every detail. Richard had been using as models the letters I had written him for the last three years, and had constructed a set of love letters from me to him, in perfect imitation of my handwriting. They compared the letters and read snatches of the sentences aloud. The letters referred constantly to our being married as soon as I should return from abroad, and some of them spoke of the money as belonging to us both, and that now it would come to its own without any further trouble.

"They even exhibited a marriage certificate, which, from what they said, must have been made out with our names, and Mrs. Chambray and the doctor signed their names as witnesses. As nearly as I could make out, they were going to use this as evidence that Richard was my husband, and that he had the right to administer my estate during the time that I was incapable. They had even arranged that a young woman who was hopelessly insane should take my place when the executors of the estate came to see me, if they took the trouble to do that. As it was some years since either of them had seen me, they could easily have been deceived. And for their help Mrs. Chambray and the doctor were to receive a handsome sum.

"I could scarcely believe my ears at first. It seemed to me that I must be mistaken, that they could not be talking about me. But my name was mentioned again and again, and as each link in the horrible plot was made plain to me, my terror grew so great that I was on the verge of rushing into the car and calling for the conductor and porter to help me. But something held me still, and I heard Richard say that he had just informed the trainmen that I was insane, and that they need not be surprised if I had to be restrained. He had told them that I was comparatively harmless, but he had no doubt that the conductor had whispered it to our fellow-passengers in the car, which explained their prolonged absence in the smoker. Then they all laughed, and it seemed to me that the cover to the bottomless pit was open and that I was falling in.

"I sat still, hardly daring to breathe. Then I began to go over the story bit by bit, and to put together little things that had happened since we landed, and even before I had left Vienna; and I saw that I was caught in a trap. It would be no use to appeal to any one, for no one would believe me. I looked wildly out at the ground and had desperate thoughts of climbing over the rail and jumping from the train. Death would be better than what I should soon have to face. My persecutors had even told how they had deceived my friends at home by sending telegrams of my mental condition, and of the necessity for putting me into an asylum. There would be no hope of appealing to them for help. The only witnesses to my sanity were far away in Vienna, and how could I reach them if I were in Richard's power?

"I watched the names of the stations as they flew by, but it gradually grew dark, and I could hardly make them out. I thought one looked like the name of a Philadelphia suburb, but I could not be sure.

"I was freezing with horror and with cold, but did not dare to move, lest I attract their attention.

"We began to rush past rows of houses, and I knew we were approaching a city. Then, suddenly, the train slowed down and stopped, with very little warning, as if it intended to halt only a second and then hurry on.

"There was a platform on one side of the train, but we were out beyond the car-shed, for our train was long. I could not climb over the rail to the platform, for I was sitting on the side away from the station, and would have had to pass the car door in order to do so. I should be sure to be seen.

"On the other side were a great many tracks separated by strong picket fences as high as the car platform and close to the trains, and they reached as far as I could see in either direction. I had no time to think, and there was nothing I could do but climb over the rail and get across those tracks and fences somehow.

"My hands were so cold and trembling that I could scarcely hold on to the rail as I jumped over.

"I cannot remember how I got across. Twice I had to cling to a fence while an express train rushed by, and the shock and noise almost stunned me. It was a miracle that I was not killed, but I did not think of that until afterwards. I was conscious only of the train I had left standing by the station. I glanced back once, and thought I saw Richard come to the door of the car. Then I stumbled on blindly. I don't remember any more until I found myself hurrying along that dark passage under the bridge and saw you just ahead. I was afraid to speak to you, but I did not know what else to do, and you were so good to me———!" Her voice broke in a little sob.

All the time she had been talking, he had held her hand firmly. She had forgotten that any one might be watching; he did not care.

The tall girl with the discontented upper lip went to the matron and told her that she thought the man and the woman in the parlor ought to be made to go. She believed the man was trying to coax the girl to do something she didn't want to do. The matron started on a voyage of discovery up the hall and down again, with penetrating glances into the room, but the two did not see her.

"Oh, my poor dear little girl!" breathed the man. "And you have passed through all this awful experience alone! Why did you not tell me about it? I could have helped you. I am a lawyer."

"I thought you would be on your guard at once and watch for evidences of my insanity. I thought perhaps you would believe it true, and would feel it necessary to return me to my friends. I think I should have been tempted to do that, perhaps, if any one had come to me with such a story."

"One could not do that after seeing and talking with you. I never could have believed it. Surely no reputable physician would lend his influence to put you in an asylum, yet I know such things have been done. Your cousin must be a desperate character. I shall not feel safe until you belong to me. I saw two men hanging about Mr. Phillips's house last evening as I went in. They were looking up at the windows and talking about keeping a close watch on some one named Mary. One of the men was tall and slight and handsome, with dark hair and eyes; the other was

Irish, and wore a coat too large for him, and rubbers. I went back later in the evening, and the Irishman was hovering about the house."

The girl looked up with frightened eyes and grasped the arms of her chair excitedly.

"Will you go with me now to a church not far away, where a friend of mine is the pastor, and be married? Then we can defy all the cousins in creation. Can't you trust me?" he pleaded.

"Oh, yes, but——"

"Is it that you do not love me?"

"No," she said, and her eyes drooped shyly. "It seems strange that I dare to say it to you when I have known you so little." She lifted her eyes, full of a wonderful love light, and she was glorified to him, all meanly dressed though she was. The smooth Madonna braids around the shapely head, covered by the soft felt hat, seemed more beautiful to him than all the elaborate head-dresses of modern times.

"Where is the 'but' then, dear? Shall we go now?"

"How can I go in this dress?" She looked down at her shabby shoes, rough black gown, and cheap gloves in dismay, and a soft pink stole into her face.

"You need not. Your own gown is out in the office in my suit-case. I brought it with me, thinking you might need it—*hoping* you might, I mean;" and he smiled. "I have kept it always near me; partly because I wanted the comfort of it, partly because I was afraid some one else might find it, and desecrate our secret with their commonplace wondering."

It was at this moment that the matron of the building stepped up to the absorbed couple, resolved to do her duty. Her lips were pursed to their thinnest, and displeasure was in her face.

The young man arose and asked in a grave tone:

"Excuse me, but can you tell me whether this lady can

get a room here to rest for a short time, while I go out and attend to a matter of business?"

The matron noticed his refined face and true eyes, and she accepted with a good grace the ten-dollar bill he handed to her.

"We charge only fifty cents a night for a room," she said, glancing at the humble garments of the man's companion. She thought the girl must be a poor dependent or a country relative.

"That's all right," said the young man. "Just let the change help the good work along."

That made a distinct change in the atmosphere. The matron smiled, and retired to snub the girl with the discontented upper lip. Then she sent the elevator boy to carry the girl's suit-case. As the matron came back to the office, a baggy man with cushioned tires hustled out of the open door into the street, having first cast back a keen, furtive glance that searched every corner of the place.

"Now," said Dunham reassuringly, as the matron disappeared, "you can go up to your room and get ready, and I will look after a few little matters. I called on my friend, the minister, this morning, and I have looked up the legal part of this affair. I can see that everything is all right in a few minutes. Is there anything you would like me to do for you?"

"No," she answered, looking up half frightened; "but I am afraid I ought not to let you do this. You scarcely know me."

"Now, dear, no more of that. We have no time to lose. How long will it take you to get dressed? Will half an hour do? It is getting late."

"Oh, it will not take long." She caught her breath with gladness. Her companion's voice was so strong and comforting, his face so filled with a wonderful love, that she felt dazed with the sudden joy of it all.

The elevator boy appeared in the doorway with the familiar suit-case.

"Don't be afraid, dear heart," whispered the young man, as he attended her to the elevator. "I'll soon be back again, and then, *then,* we shall be together!"

It was a large front room to which the boy took her. The ten-dollar bill had proven effective. It was not a "fifty-cents-a-night" room. Some one—some guest or kindly patron—had put a small illuminated text upon the wall in a neat frame. It met her eye as she entered—"Rejoice and be glad." Just a common little picture card, it was, with a phrase that had become trite to many, yet it seemed a message to her, and her heart leaped to obey. She went to the window to catch a glimpse of the man who would soon be her husband, but he was not there, and the hurrying people reminded her that she must hasten. Across the street a slouching figure in a baggy coat looked fixedly up and caught her glance. She trembled and drew back out of the sunshine, remembering what Dunham had told her about the Irishman of the night before. With a quick instinct, she drew down the shade, and locked her door.

12

THE rubbered feet across the way hurried their owner into the cigar-store in front of which he had been standing, and where he had a good view of the Y.W.C.A. Building. He flung down some change and demanded the use of the telephone. Then, with one eye on the opposite doorway, he called up a number and delivered his message.

"Oi've treed me bird. She's in a room allroight at the Y.W.C.A. place, fer I seed her at the winder. She come with a foine gintlemin, but he's gahn now, an' she's loike to stay a spell. You'd best come at once. . . . All roight. Hurry up!" He hung up the telephone-receiver and hurried back to his post in front of the big entrance. Meanwhile the bride-elect upstairs, with happy heart and trembling fingers, was putting on her own beautiful garments once more, and arranging the waves of lovely hair in their old accustomed way.

Tryon Dunham's plans were well laid. He first called up his friend the minister and told him to be ready; then a florist not far from the church; then a large department store where he had spent some time that morning. "Is that Mr. Hunter, head of the fur department? Mr. Hunter, this is Mr. Dunham. You remember our conversation this morning? Kindly send the coat and hat I selected to the Y.W.C.A. Building at once. Yes, just send them to the office. You remember it was to be C.O.D., and I showed you my certified check this morning. It's all right, is it? How long will it take you to get it there? ... All right. Have the boy wait if I'm not there. Good-by."

His next move was to order a carriage, and have it stop at the florist's on the way. That done, he consulted his watch. Seventeen minutes of his precious half-hour were gone. With nervous haste he went into a telephone booth and called up his own home on the long-distance.

To his relief, his mother answered.

"Is that you, Mother? This is Tryon. Are you all well? That's good. Yes, I'm in Chicago, but will soon be home. Mother, I've something to tell you that may startle you, though there is nothing to make you sad. You have known that there was something on my mind for some time." He paused for the murmur of assent.

He knew how his mother was looking, even though he could not see her—that set look of being ready for anything. He wanted to spare her as much as possible, so he hastened on:

"You remember speaking to me about the ring I wore?"

"Tryon! Are you engaged?" There was a sharp anxiety in the tone as it came through the hundreds of miles of space.

"One better, Mother. I'm just about to be married!"

"My son! What have you done? Don't forget the honorable name you bear!"

"No, Mother, I don't forget. She's fine and beautiful and sweet. You will love her, and our world will fall at her feet!"

"But who is she? You must remember that love is very blind. Tryon, you must come home at once. I shall die if you disgrace us all. Don't do anything to spoil our lives. I know it is something dreadful, or you would not do it in such haste."

"Nothing of the kind, Mother. Can't you trust me? Let me explain. She is alone, and legal circumstances which it would take too long for me to explain over the 'phone have made it desirable for her to have my immediate protection. We are going at once to Edwin Twinell's church, and he will marry us. It is all arranged, but I felt that you ought to be told beforehand. We shall probably take the night express for home. Tell Cornelia that I shall expect congratulations telegraphed to the hotel here inside of two hours."

"But, Tryon, what will our friends think? It is most extraordinary! How can you manage about announcements?"

"Bother the red tape, Mother! What difference does that make? Put it in the society column if you want to."

"But, Tryon, we do not want to be conspicuous!"

"Well, Mother, I'm not going to put off my wedding at the last minute for a matter of some bits of pasteboard. I'll do any reasonable thing to please you, but not that."

"Couldn't you get a chaperon for her, and bring her on to me? Then we could plan the wedding at our leisure."

"Impossible, Mother! In the first place, she never would consent. Really, I cannot talk any more about it. I must go at once, or I shall be late. Tell me you will love her for my sake, until you love her for her own."

"Tryon, you always were unreasonable. Suppose you have the cards engraved at once, and I will telegraph our list to the engraver if you will give me his address. If you prefer, you can get them engraved and sent out from there. That will keep tongues still."

"All right, I'll do it. I'll have the engraver telegraph his address to you within two hours. Have your list ready.

And, Mother, don't worry. She's all right. You couldn't have chosen better yourself. Say you will love her, Mother dear."

"Oh, I suppose I'll try," sighed the wires disconsolately; "but I never thought you would be married in such a way. Why, you haven't even told me who she is."

"She's all right, Mother—good family and all. I really must hurry——"

"But what is her name, Tryon?"

"Say, Mother, I really must go. Ask Mrs. Parker Bowman what she thinks of her. Good-by! Cheer up, it'll be all right."

"But, Tryon, her name——"

The receiver was hung up with a click, and Dunham looked at his watch nervously. In two minutes his half-hour would be up, yet he must let Judge Blackwell know. Perhaps he could still catch him at the office. He sometimes stayed down-town late. Dunham rang up the office. The Judge was still there, and in a moment his cheery voice was heard ringing out, "Hello!"

"Hello, Judge! Is that you? . . . This is Dunham. . . . Chicago. Yes, the business is all done, and I'm ready to come home, but I want to give you a bit of news. Do you remember the young woman who dined with us at Mrs. Bowman's and played the piano so well? . . . Yes, the night I met you. . . . Well, you half guessed that night how it was with us, I think. And now she is here, and we are to be married at once, before I return. I am just about to go to the church, but I wanted your blessing first."

"Blessings and congratulations on you both!" came in a hearty voice over the phone. "Tell her she shall be at once taken into the firm as chief consultant on condition that she plays for me whenever I ask her."

A great gladness entered the young man's heart as he again hung up the receiver, at this glimpse into the bright vista of future possibilities. He hurried into the street, forgetful of engravers. The half-hour was up and one minute over.

In the meantime, the girl had slipped into her own garments once more with a relief and joy she could scarcely believe were her own. Had it all been an ugly dream, this life she had been living for the past few months, and was she going back now to rest and peace and real life? Nay, not going back, but going forward. The sweet color came into her beautiful face at the thought of the one who, though not knowing her, yet had loved her enough to take her as she was, and lift her out of her trouble. It was like the most romantic of fairy tales, this unexpected lover and the joy that had come to her. How had it happened to her quiet, conventional life? Ah, it was good and dear, whatever it was! She pressed her happy eyes with her fluttering, nervous fingers, to keep the glad tears back, and laughed out to herself a joyful ripple such as she had not uttered since her uncle's death.

A knock at the door brought her back to realities again. Her heart throbbed wildly. Had he come back to her already? Or had her enemy found her out at last?

Tryon Dunham hurried up the steps of the Y.W.C.A. Building, nearly knocking over a baggy individual in rubbers, who was lurking in the entrance. The young man had seen a boy in uniform, laden with two enormous boxes, run up the steps as he turned the last corner. Hastily writing a few lines on one of his cards and slipping it into the largest box, he sent them both up to the girl's room. Then he sauntered to the door to see if the carriage had come. It was there. He glanced inside to see if his orders about flowers had been fulfilled, and spoke a few words of direction to the driver. Turning back to the door, he found the small, red eyes of the baggy Irishman fixed upon him. Something in the slouch of the figure reminded Dunham strongly now of the man he had noticed the night before, and as he went back into the building he looked the man over well and determined to watch him. As he sat in the office waiting, twice he saw the bleary eyes of the baggy man applied to the glass panes in the front door and as suddenly withdrawn. It irritated him, and finally he strode to the door and asked the man if he were looking for some one.

"Just waitin' fer me sweetheart," whined the man, with a cringing attitude. "She has a room in here, an' I saw her go in a while back."

"Well, you'd better move on. They don't care to have people hanging around here."

The man slunk away with a vindictive glance, and Tryon Dunham went back to the office, more perturbed at the little incident than he could understand.

Upstairs the girl had dared to open her door and had been relieved to find the elevator boy there with the two boxes.

"The gentleman's below, an' he says he'll wait, an' he sent these up," said the boy, depositing his burden and hurrying away.

She locked her door once more, for somehow a great fear had stolen over her now that she was again dressed in her own garments and could easily be recognized.

She opened the large box and read the card lying on the top:

> These are my wedding gifts to you, Dear. Put them on and come as soon as possible to the one who loves you better than anything else in life.
> Tryon

Her eyes shone brightly and her cheeks grew rosy red as she lifted out from its tissue-paper wrappings a long, rich coat of Alaska seal, with exquisite brocade lining. She put it on and stood a moment looking at herself in the glass. She felt like one who had for a long time lost her identity, and has suddenly had it restored. Such garments had been ordinary comforts of her former life. She had not been warm enough in the coarse black coat.

The other box contained a beautiful hat of fur to match the coat. It was simply trimmed with one long, beautiful black plume, and in shape and general appearance was like the hat he had borrowed for her use in the fall. She smiled happily as she set it upon her head, and then laughed outright as she remembered her shabby silk gloves. Never mind. She could take them off when she reached the church.

She packed the little black dress into the suit-case, folded the felt hat on the top with a tender pat, and, putting on her gloves, hurried down to the one who waited for her.

The matron had gone upstairs to the linen closet and left the girl with the discontented upper lip in charge in the office. The latter watched the elegant lady in the rich furs come down the hall from the elevator, and wondered who she was and why she had been upstairs. Probably to visit some poor protégée, she thought. The girl caught the love-light in the eyes of Tryon Dunham as he rose to meet his bride, and she recognized him as the same man who had been in close converse with the cheaply dressed girl in the parlor an hour before, and sneered as she wondered what the fine lady in furs would think if she knew about the other girl. Then they went out to the carriage, past the baggy, rubbered man, who shrank back suddenly behind a stone column and watched them.

As Dunham shut the door, he looked back just in time to see a slight man, with dark eyes and hair, hurry up and touch the baggy man on the shoulder. The latter pointed toward their carriage.

"See!" said Dunham. "I believe those are the men who were hovering around the house last night."

The girl leaned forward to look, and then drew back with an exclamation of horror as the carriage started.

"Oh, that man is my cousin Richard," she cried.

"Are you sure?" he asked, and a look of determination settled into his face.

"Perfectly," she answered, looking out again. "Do you suppose he has seen me?"

"I suppose he has, but we'll soon turn the tables." He leaned out and spoke a word to the driver, who drew up around the next corner in front of a telephone pay-station.

"Come with me for just a minute, dear. I'll telephone to a detective bureau where they know me and have that man watched. He is unsafe to have at large." He helped her out and drew her arm firmly within his own. "Don't be afraid any more. I will take care of you."

He telephoned a careful description of the two men and their whereabouts, and before he had hung up the receiver a man had started post-haste for the Y.W.C.A. Building.

Then Tryon Dunham put the girl tenderly into the carriage, and to divert her attention he opened the box of flowers and put a great sheaf of white roses and lilies-of-the-valley into the little gloved hands. Then, taking her in his arms for the first time, he kissed her. He noticed the shabby gloves, and, putting his hand in his breast pocket, drew out the white gloves she had worn before, saying, "See! I have carried them there ever since you sent them back! My sister never asked for them. I kept them for your sake."

The color had come back into her cheeks when they reached the church, and he thought her a beautiful bride as he led her into the dim aisle. Some one up in the choir loft was playing the wedding march, and the minister's wife and young daughter sat waiting to witness the ceremony.

The minister met them at the door with a welcoming smile and hand-shake, and led them forward. As the music hushed for the words of the ceremony, he leaned forward to the young man and whispered:

"I neglected to ask you her name, Tryon."

"Oh, yes." The young man paused in his dilemma and looked for an instant at the sweet face of the girl beside him. But he could not let his friend see that he did not know the name of his wife-to-be, and with quick thought he answered, "Mary!"

The ceremony proceeded, and the minister's voice sounded out solemnly in the empty church: "Do you, Tryon, take this woman whom you hold by the hand to be your lawful wedded wife?"

The young man's fingers held the timid hand of the woman firmly as he answered, "I do."

"Do you, Mary, take this man?" came the next question, and the girl looked up with clear eyes and said, "I do."

Then the minister's wife, who knew and prized Tryon Dunham's friendship, said to herself: "It's all right. She loves him."

When the solemn words were spoken that bound them together through life, and they had thanked their kind friends and were once more out in the carriage, Tryon said:

"Do you know you haven't told me your real name yet?"

She laughed happily as the carriage started on its way, and answered, "Why, it is Mary!"

As the carriage rounded the first corner beyond the church, two breathless individuals hurried up from the other direction. One was short and baggy, and the sole of one rubber flopped dismally as he struggled to keep up with the alert strides of the other man, who was slim and angry. They had been detained by an altercation with the matron of the Y.W.C.A. Building, and puzzled by the story of the plainly dressed girl who had taken the room, and the fine lady who had left the building in company with a gentleman, until it was settled by the elevator boy, who declared the two women to be one and the same.

A moment later a man in citizen's clothing, who had

keen eyes, and who was riding a motor-cycle, rounded the corner and puffed placidly along near the two. He appeared to be looking at the numbers on the other side of the street, but he heard every word that they said as they caught sight of the disappearing carriage and hurried after it. He had been standing in the entrance of the Y.W.C.A. Building, an apparently careless observer, while the elevator boy gave his evidence.

The motor-cycle shot ahead a few rods, passed the carriage, and discovered by a keen glance who were the occupants. Then it rounded the block and came almost up to the two pursuers again.

When the carriage stopped at the side entrance of a hotel the man on the motor-cycle was ahead of the pursuers and discovered it first, long enough to see the two get out and go up the marble steps. The carriage was driving away when the thin man came in sight, with the baggy man struggling along half a block behind, his padded feet coming down in heavy, dragging thuds, like a St. Bernard dog in bedroom slippers.

One glimpse the pursuers had of their prey as the elevator shot upward. They managed to evade the hotel authorities and get up the wide staircase without observation. By keeping on the alert, they discovered that the elevator had stopped at the second floor, so the people they were tracking must have apartments there. Lurking in the shadowy parts of the hall, they watched, and soon were rewarded by seeing Dunham come out of a room and hurry to the elevator. He had remembered his promise to his mother about the engravers. As soon as he was gone they presented themselves boldly at the door.

Filled with the joy that had come to her and feeling entirely safe now in the protection of her husband, Mary Dunham opened the door. She supposed, of course, it was the bell-boy with a pitcher of ice-water, for which she had just rung.

"Ah, here you are at last, my pretty cousin!" It was the voice of Richard that menaced her, with all the stored-up wrath of his long-baffled search.

At that moment the man from the motor-cycle stepped softly up the top stair and slid unseen into the shadows of the hall.

For an instant it seemed to Mary Dunham that she was going to faint, and in one swift flash of thought she saw herself overpowered and carried into hiding before her husband should return. But with a supreme effort she controlled herself, and faced her tormentor with unflinching gaze. Though her strength had deserted her at first, every faculty was now keen and collected. As if nothing unusual were happening, she put out her cold, trembling fingers, and laid them firmly over the electric button on the wall. Then with new strength coming from the certainty that some one would soon come to her aid, she opened her lips to speak.

"What are you doing here, Richard?"

"I've come after you, my lady. A nice chase you've led me, but you shall pay for it now."

The cruelty in his face eclipsed any lines of beauty which might have been there. The girl's heart froze within her as she looked once more into those eyes, which had always seemed to her like sword-points.

"I shall never go anywhere with you," she answered steadily.

He seized her delicate wrist roughly, twisting it with the old wrench with which he had tormented her in their childhood days. None of them saw the stranger who was quietly walking down the hall toward them.

"Will you go peaceably, or shall I have to gag and bind you?" said Richard. "Choose quickly. I'm in no mood to trifle with you any longer."

Although he hurt her wrist cruelly, she threw herself back from him and with her other hand pressed still harder against the electric button. The bell was ringing furiously down in the office, but the walls were thick and the halls lofty. It could not be heard above.

"Catch that other hand, Mike," commanded Richard, "and stuff this in her mouth, while I tie her hands behind her back."

It was then that Mary screamed. The man in the shadow stepped up behind and said in a low voice:

"What does all this mean?"

The two men, startled, dropped the girl's hands for the instant. Then Richard, white with anger at this interference, answered insolently: "It means that this girl's an escaped lunatic, and we're sent to take her back. She's dangerous, so you'd better keep out of the way."

Then Mary Dunham's voice, clear and penetrating, rang through the halls:

"Tryon, Tryon! Come quick! Help! Help!"

As if in answer to her call, the elevator shot up to the second floor, and Tryon Dunham stepped out in time to see the two men snatch Mary's hands again and attempt to bind them behind her back.

In an instant he had seized Richard by the collar and landed him on the hall carpet, while a well directed blow sent the flabby Irishman sprawling at the feet of the detective, who promptly sat on him and pinioned his arms behind him.

"How dare you lay a finger upon this lady?" said Tryon Dunham, as he stepped to the side of his wife and put a strong arm about her, where she stood white and frightened in the doorway.

No one had noticed that the bell-boy had come to the head of the stairs and received a quiet order from the detective.

In sudden fear, the discomfited Richard arose and attempted to bluff the stranger who had so unwarrantly interfered just as his fingers were about to close over the golden treasure of his cousin's fortune.

"Indeed, sir, you wholly misunderstand the situation," he said to Dunham, with an air of injured innocence, "though perhaps you can scarcely be blamed. This girl is an escaped lunatic. We have been searching for her for days, and have just traced her. It is our business to take her back at once. Her friends are in great distress about her. Moreover, she is dangerous and a menace to every guest in this house. She has several times attempted murder——"

"Stop!" roared Dunham, in a thunderous voice of righteous anger. "She is my wife. And you are her cousin. I know all about your plot to shut her up in an insane asylum and steal her fortune. I have found you sooner than I expected, and I intend to see that the law takes its full course with you."

Two policemen now arrived on the scene, with a number of eager bell-boys and porters in their wake, ready to take part in the excitement.

Richard had turned deadly white at the words, "She is my wife!" It was the death-knell of his hopes of securing the fortune for which he had not hesitated to sacrifice every particle of moral principle. When he turned and saw impending retribution in the shape of the two stalwart representatives of the law, a look of cunning came into his face, and with one swift motion he turned to flee up the staircase close at hand.

"Not much you don't," said an enterprising bell-boy, flinging himself in the way and tripping up the scoundrel in his flight.

The policemen were upon him and had him handcuffed in an instant. The Irishman now began to protest that he was but an innocent tool, hired to help discover the whereabouts of an escaped lunatic, as he supposed. He was walked off to the patrol wagon without further ceremony.

It was all over in a few minutes. The elevator carried off the detective, the policemen, and their two prisoners. The door closed behind Dunham and his bride, and the curious guests who had peered out, alarmed by the uproar, saw nothing but a few bell-boys standing in the hall, describing to one another the scene as they had witnessed it.

"He stood here and I stood right there," said one, "and the policeman, he come——"

The guests could not find out just what had happened, but supposed there had been an attempted robbery, and retired behind locked doors to see that their jewels were safely hidden.

Dunham drew the trembling girl into his arms and tried to soothe her. The tears rained down the white cheeks as her head lay upon his breast, and he kissed them away.

"Oh!" she sobbed, shuddering. "If you had not come! It was terrible, *terrible!* I believe he would have killed me rather than have let me go again."

Gradually his tender ministrations calmed her, but she turned troubled eyes to his face.

"You do not know yet that I am all I say. You have nothing to prove it. Of course, by and by, when I can get to my guardians, and with your help perhaps make them understand, you will know, but I don't see how you can trust me till then."

For answer he brought his hand up in front of her face and turned the flashing diamond—her diamond—so that its glory caught the single ray of the setting sun that filtered into the hotel window.

"See, darling," he said. "It is your ring. I have worn it ever since as an outward sign that I trusted you."

"You are taking me on trust, though, in spite of all you say, and it is beautiful."

He laid his lips against hers. "Yes," he said; "it is beautiful, and it is best."

It was very still in the room for a moment while she

nestled close to him and his eyes drank in the sweetness of her face.

"See," said he, taking a tiny velvet case from his pocket and touching the spring that opened it. "I have amused myself finding a mate to your stone. I thought perhaps you would let me wear your ring always, while you wear mine."

He lifted the jewel from its white velvet bed and showed her the inscription inside: "Mary, from Tryon." Then he slipped it on her finger to guard the wedding ring he had given her at the church. His arm that encircled her clasped her left wrist, and the two diamonds flashed side by side. The last gleam of the setting sun, ere it vanished behind the tall buildings on the west, glanced in and blazed the gems into tangled beams of glory, darting out in many colored prisms to light the vision of the future of the man and the woman. He bent and kissed her again, and their eyes met like other jewels, in which gleamed the glory of their love and trust.

Don't miss these Grace Livingston Hill romance novels!

VOL.	TITLE	ORDER NUM.	PRICE
1	Where Two Ways Met	07-8203-8-HILC	3.95
2	Bright Arrows	07-0380-4-HILC	3.95
3	A Girl to Come Home To	07-1017-7-HILC	3.95
4	Amorelle	07-0310-3-HILC	3.95
5	Kerry	07-2044-X-HILC	4.95
6	All Through the Night	07-0018-X-HILC	4.95
7	The Best Man	07-0371-5-HILC	3.95
8	Ariel Custer	07-1686-8-HILC	3.95
9	The Girl of the Woods	07-1016-9-HILC	3.95
11	More Than Conqueror	07-4559-0-HILC	3.95
12	Head of the House	07-1309-5-HILC	4.95
14	Stranger within the Gates	07-6441-2-HILC	3.95
15	Marigold	07-4037-8-HILC	3.95
16	Rainbow Cottage	07-5731-0-HILC	4.95
17	Maris	07-4042-4-HILC	4.95
18	Brentwood	07-0364-2-HILC	4.95
19	Daphne Deane	07-0529-7-HILC	3.95
20	The Substitute Guest	07-6447-1-HILC	3.95
28	White Orchids	07-8150-3-HILC	4.95
63	The Man of the Desert	07-3955-8-HILC	3.95
64	Miss Lavinia's Call	07-4360-1-HILC	3.95
77	The Ransom	07-5143-4-HILC	3.95
78	Found Treasure	07-0911-X-HILC	3.95
79	The Big Blue Soldier	07-0374-X-HILC	3.50
80	The Challengers	07-0362-6-HILC	3.95
81	Duskin	07-0574-2-HILC	4.95
82	The White Flower	07-8149-X-HILC	4.95
83	Marcia Schuyler	07-4036-X-HILC	4.95
84	Cloudy Jewel	07-0474-6-HILC	4.95
85	Crimson Mountain	07-0472-X-HILC	4.95
86	The Mystery of Mary	07-4632-5-HILC	3.95
87	Out of the Storm	07-4778-X-HILC	3.95
88	Phoebe Deane	07-5033-0-HILC	4.95
89	Re-Creations	07-5334-8-HILC	4.95
90	Sound of the Trumpet	07-6107-3-HILC	4.95
91	A Voice in the Wilderness	07-7908-8-HILC	4.95

The Grace Livingston Hill romance novels are available at your local bookstore, or you may order by mail (U.S. and territories only). For your convenience, use this page to place your order or write the information on a separate sheet of paper, including the order number for each book.

Mail your order with check or money order for the price of the book plus $2.00 for postage and handling to: **Tyndale Family Products, P.O. Box 448, Wheaton, IL 60189-0448.** Allow 4-6 weeks for delivery. Prices subject to change.